Big Dark Hole

Also by Jeffrey Ford

Vanitas
The Physiognomy
Memoranda
The Beyond
The Fantasy Writer's Assistant
The Portrait of Mrs. Charbuque
The Girl in the Glass
The Cosmology of the Wider World
The Empire of Ice Cream
The Shadow Year
The Drowned Life
Crackpot Palace
A Natural History of Hell
Ahab's Return: or, The Last Voyage
The Best of Jeffrey Ford

Stories

JEFFREY FORD

Small Beer Press
Easthampton, MA

Small Beer Press
150 Pleasant Street #306
Easthampton, MA 01027
smallbeerpress.com
weightlessbooks.com
bookmoonbooks.com
info@smallbeerpress.com

Distributed to the trade by Consortium.

Library of Congress Cataloging-in-Publication Data

Names: Ford, Jeffrey, 1955- author.
Title: Big dark hole : stories / Jeffrey Ford.
Description: First edition. | Easthampton, MA : Small Beer Press, [2021] | Summary: "Jeffrey Ford's stories often start out as seemingly everyday realist and then the weird comes crashing in. Big Dark Hole is about the dark holes we might find ourselves in right now and maybe, too, those inside us"-- Provided by publisher.
Identifiers: LCCN 2020057199 (print) | LCCN 2020057200 (ebook) | ISBN 9781618731845 (paperback) | ISBN 9781618731852 (ebook)
Subjects: LCGFT: Short stories.
Classification: LCC PS3556.O6997 B54 2021 (print) | LCC PS3556.O6997 (ebook) | DDC 813/.54--dc23
LC record available at https://lccn.loc.gov/2020057199
LC ebook record available at https://lccn.loc.gov/2020057200

First edition 1 2 3 4 5 6 7 8 9

Set in Minion 12 pt.
Cover illustration: "Vanitas Still Life" by Herman Henstenburgh, Creative Commons Universal, CC0 1.0, the Met (www.metmuseum.org).

Printed on 55# Natures Natural 30% PCR recycled paper by the Versa Press in East Peoria, IL.

For Lucius Shepard, Kit Reed, and Graham Joyce.
Gone but not forgotten. Their voices and their visions
are always on a shelf nearby. I visit them often.

"To live is to be slowly born."
Antoine de Saint-Exupery

Contents

The Thousand Eyes

I doubt South Jersey's ever been called *The Land Where No One Dies,* but according to my painter friend, Barney, who lives near Dividing Creek on the edge of the marshland leading to the Delaware, back in the early '60s—out there amid the two mile stretch of cattails, quaking islands, and rivulets—there was a lounge called The Thousand Eyes, and there was a performer who sang there every Wednesday night, advertised on a hand-painted billboard along the northbound lane to Money Island as Ronnie Dunn, The Voice of Death.

Barney heard all about it from another local painter, Merle. Old Merle was getting on in years, and I'd see him, myself, when driving through Milville, creeping along the sidewalk in his tattered beret, talking to himself. He swore that his apartment was haunted. Still, Barney said he never doubted what Merle told him. The reason he trusted him was that a few years back he'd asked him if he'd ever been married. The old man said, "Once, for a few months, to a charming young blonde, Eloise. It lasted through spring and summer, but come fall she up and fled. Left me a note, saying my breath stinks and my dick's too small." Barney vouched for the former, and then added "Do you think somebody who'd tell you something like that would lie to you?"

Anyway. Merle was in his late 20s and it was 1966. He was living by himself in the top-floor apartment of a half-abandoned building in the town of Shell Pile. Even though the floorboards creaked, the paint curled, the windows let in the cold, and every hinge groaned, the place was big, with plenty of room to paint and live. He scrounged together an existence between doing odd jobs around town and working a few shifts when he had to loading trucks at the sand factory. If he had to travel any distance, he rode a rusted old bike with a basket and pedal brakes. He ate very little, twice a day, and blew most of his income on cigarettes, liquor, and weed. The most important thing to him was that he had plenty of time to paint. As long as he had that, he was happy.

At the time, he was working on a series of paintings depicting the bars in South Jersey. He'd go to one, have a few drinks, take some shots with his Polaroid Swinger and then go back to his place and paint an interior scene with patrons and barkeep, bottles and bubbling neon signs. Barney explained Merle's style as "Edward Hicks meets Edward Hopper in a bare-knuckle match." Still, he was a hard worker, and before long he'd been to all the bars in the area and painted scenes from each. He liked the individual paintings in the series, but overall he felt something was missing.

Then one day when he splurged for lunch and had a burger and fries at Jack's Diner, served as they always were back then on a piece of wax paper instead of a plate, he overheard the conversation of the old couple in the booth behind his and realized what it was that was missing from his series.

"The Thousand Eyes," he heard her say, and instantly it struck him that he'd not painted it.

"I heard it's impossible to get to," the old man said.

"Nah, I had Doris at the liquor store draw me a map."

"That's where you want to go for our fortieth, some mildewed old cocktail lounge sinking into the Delaware?"

"I want to hear that singer who's there on Wednesday night, Ronnie Dunn. He's got a record that they play on the local station 'Fond Wanderer.'"

"Wait a second," he said. "That's the 'word of doom' guy."

"The Voice of Death."

"Who wants to hear the voice of death?" he said.

"You know, it's a gimmick. Mysterious."

Their food came then and Merle paid and left.

He'd heard about the Thousand Eyes since he'd moved to Shell Pile, but he'd never been there. It advertised only late at night on the local radio with a snappy jingle, "*No one cries at the Thousand Eyes.*" The place came up in conversation around town quite often, but he'd only met a handful of people who'd actually been. The shift manager at the sand factory told him, "I drank out there one afternoon during low tide. If a shit took a shit, that's what it would smell like. I almost hallucinated."

There was a woman he met at one of the bars he was photographing who told him that she heard, and now believed, that only certain people were called to see Ronnie Dunn perform. The singer sent out secret invitations through his song on the radio. If one was for you, you would find the Thousand Eyes; if not, you wouldn't. "I've been out there three times with my girlfriends, and three times we got lost," she said. "A couple of people supposedly went to look for it and never came back."

"Is that true?" asked Merle.

"I guess so," she said.

Luckily, Doris at the liquor store didn't mind at all drawing Merle a map.

So on a Wednesday night in September, he took off on his bike, camera around his neck, pedaling west toward the river. Doris figured by bike the trip would take him about an hour and a half. He was to look for Frog Road off Jericho, and then head west following Glass Eel Creek, looking for a spot where a packed-dirt path led off on the right into the cattails and bramble. She told him the Army Corps of Engineers built the road back in the early '50s when they were trying to eradicate mosquitos. The sunset was rich in pink and the weather was cool.

Merle rode fast, excited by the prospect of finally finishing what he'd started.

He found the path and took it out into the marsh, cutting through stretches of cattail, stretches of soggy earth dotted with green. He passed into a small wood, all its trees twisted and stunted by the salt content in the water. Stopping and resting for a moment, he took a deep breath. The call of mourning doves and the breeze in the dying leaves gave him a chill of loneliness. As he got back to pedaling, he wondered how lonely it would feel there in the dark on the way home. On the other side of a clutch of white sand dunes, he descended and crossed a wooden bridge over what looked like deep water. Beyond it sat the Thousand Eyes, majestic in its grandiose molder. A Victorian structure with a wraparound porch and a splintering wooden cupola over the entrance.

The dirt path became the dirt parking lot of the place. Situated at the spot where one turned into the other there was a large sign held up by two 4x4's planted in the ground. The only writing it held was in the very bottom right corner; otherwise it was a big rectangle of eyes on a violet background. Carefully rendered peepers of all sizes with lids and lashes, staring, squinting, popping and red, sad and blue. In the corner it said, "These one thousand eyes were painted by Lew Pharo." Pharo was one of the local painters, and Merle knew him. He couldn't recall Lew ever speaking of this job, though.

Beneath the signature, there was a vertical list in smaller script—No Bare Feet, No Pets, No Foul Language, No Spitting, No Cameras! Merle hid his bike in the cattails at the edge of the parking lot and then took his jacket off and wrapped it around the camera. Darkness swamped the marsh as he took the splintered steps to the entrance. He opened the glass door, and when he closed it the sound echoed through the place. His footsteps set the floorboards to squealing down a dim hallway. Off to his right, he saw a pair of doors flung open on a large room lined on two sides by windows. A lit tea candle sat on every table, and beyond there was a dance floor and a low stage with a curtain behind it. As he entered, the bar came into view off to the left.

There was a guy behind it wearing a white shirt with the sleeves rolled up and a black bow tie. He had a lit cigarette in the corner of his mouth. When he caught sight of Merle, he called in a puff of smoke, "Step right up." An older man and woman sat at the bar, drinking martinis. "What'll it be, sailor?" the bartender said.

"Vodka on the rocks," said Merle.

"A purist."

"Is Ronnie Dunn performing tonight?"

The woman turned and said "Yes" before the bartender could answer.

Merle wondered if the old couple were the same people from Jack's Diner. His drink came and he said, "So, did you name this place after the Bobby Vee song?"

"This place has been here long before that song ever came to be," said the bartender. "In fact, that song was written by two women and a guy. The guy, Ben Weisman, who wrote songs for Elvis and dozens of other stars, came in here one night, and that's where they got the title for 'The Night Has a Thousand Eyes.'"

"For real?" said Merle.

"Yeah, there was this housewife from Passaic, Florence Greenberg, who started a record company around 1960, Tiara Records. She was on vacation down here that summer, visiting relatives, and Weisman flew into Philly and drove down here to try to sell her some songs for her artists. Greenberg's niece, Doris, gave them directions to the Thousand Eyes as a place to get away, and they spent the afternoon into the night, doing business right at this bar. I was tending bar that night, and I clearly remember Weisman at one point asking Greenberg, 'What rhymes with eyes?'" The bartender took a deep drag on his cigarette to emphasize the profundity and blew it out at the ceiling.

After another round had been served, the bartender said, "You folks better get your seats for the show. It's gonna get crowded in here in a few minutes." Merle thanked him, took his drink and balled-up jacket, and chose a table set off in the back by the wall from where he could take the whole scene in at once. He sat there, staring into the light of the candle on the table, sipping his vodka, feeling for the first time the damp chill of the place, when a thought popped into his head. First it struck him that he hadn't seen Lew Pharo in a long while, and then came the memory flash that Pharo was, in fact, dead. It all came back—Lew had suddenly gone blind, couldn't paint, and shot himself in the head.

He smelled low tide, heard the cars pull up in the parking lot. The patrons shuffled in. That night the Thousand Eyes drew six couples in rumpled finery, a pair of girls a little younger than Merle, a creepy-looking guy with a wicked underbite, and a crazy woman in flowing pink gauze who danced to her chair. A waiter appeared and took orders. Merle was still trying to figure out, since he had to use the flash, how he was going to get a shot. He wondered how serious they were about No Cameras.

By 8:30, everyone was juiced. The waiter had been twice to Merle's table and the bartender put on the jukebox a string of Jay Black and the Americans tunes. The crazy lady in pink and the guy with the underbite took to the dance floor and did a dramatic fake tango to "Cara Mia" and everybody applauded. Finally at 9:00, the house lights went down, and then out. A few moments later a spotlight appeared on the 12-inch raised platform at the edge of the dance floor. It was the waiter with a microphone hooked to a small sound system strapped to a hand truck. "Ladies and gentlemen," he said into the mic, which sparked with feedback, "now the moment you've all been waiting for." While he spoke, two guys rolled a very small piano onto the stage from behind a curtain.

The waiter stepped forward as they brought out a drum set. "As some of you might know, there's an old Romanian tale about a man who, late in his life, becomes wealthy. This fellow thinks it's a shame that he won't live long enough to spend all of his money. His rich friends tell him he should go to The Land Where No One Dies. So he does and takes his wife and daughter with him. Everything there is smooth as silk, plenty of sunshine, plenty of booze, no hangovers. What's not to love? But then the wealthy man finds out that although no one dies, occasionally someone hears a persistent voice calling them. When they follow it, they never return. He realized this must be the voice of death. When his daughter hears its call, he tries to stop her from following it but he fails. The voice is just too compelling."

The waiter stopped for a deep breath and then said, "Renowned critics, ladies and gentlemen, have likened the allure of our special guest performer's voice to the voice in that very tale. So let's hear it for RRRRRRonnie DUNN, the Voice of Death." The guys moving the instruments had become the band—a bass, piano, electric guitar, and drum. They played "Smoke Gets in Your Eyes," and the stage filled with fog. It crept up around the legs of the players and billowed out onto the dance floor. When it cleared, there stood Ronnie Dunn, mic in hand. The band switched course into the intro for "Fond Wanderer."

Barney quoted to me Merle's first-hand impression of the singer. "It looked like they dredged him out of the river. Gray complexion, and kind of barnacles all over his neck and face. His hair was white going yellow like an old wedding dress, and he wore it in a moth-eaten wave. The tux was too tight. Ronnie wasn't just Dunn, he was well done." Still, he slowly lifted the mic and sang.

Fond Wanderer, where do you go?
Fond Wanderer, I know you don't know.
Fond Wanderer, come to me now,
Step into the shadow, and I'll show you how.

Merle described Dunn's voice as, "If you took Little Jimmy Scott and Big Ed Townsend and sandwiched Johnny Ray between them and then lit the whole fucking thing on fire, it'd be a little like that." He said Ronnie was out of tune and behind the count, low, menacing, but sometimes he'd hit a few sweet and beautiful notes. There was a rich resonance to its sound before it even hit the twang of the tinny speaker, like a song echoing down through a metal pipe from some strange other place. Off-putting at first, then intriguing, and eventually its appeal was hard to resist.

Fond Wanderer, please hear my plea.
Fond Wanderer, you can't ignore me.
Fond Wanderer, it's over and out,
More like a whimper, less like a shout.

Ronnie creaked around with some mortuary footwork between stanzas and then hopped off the stage and approached the table with the two young women. "You girls busy tonight?" he said into the mic. The band waited for him, keeping the tune going. "Step into the shadow," he said, "and I'll show you how." The young women grimaced, got up and left. The crowd loved it.

Fond Wanderer, can I have this dance?
Fond Wanderer, are you sleepy by chance?
Fond Wanderer, this way's the door,
Out to the boat waiting down by the shore.

Merle heard the song on the radio enough to know there was another stanza coming. He got the camera and put his jacket on. His strategy, born from momentary intuition, was to approach from the right, sweeping around the tables to that side and getting close to the stage from where he could capture Ronnie, some of the patrons on the dance floor, and the reflection of the tea candles off the mirror and bottles behind the bar. He moved without hesitation.

The flash made the singer lift his arm in front of his eyes and stagger backward, shrieking like a gull. In the fifteen seconds Merle had to let the film develop before he could rip it off and peel it open, the band stopped playing and Ronnie lurched through the spotlight. "You've ruined it," he screamed, going green in the face. Dust fell out of his nose and his hair wave had broken. Abruptly he stopped, looked across to the bartender and yelled, "Don't just stand there, get the camera. Come on." The bartender waved to the guys in the band and they put down their instruments and stood up. Merle ran.

He brushed past the couples on the dance floor and was heading toward the double doors. From the corner of his eye he noticed the bartender coming from behind the bar with a sap in his hand. He looked to the doors again, only to find that the waiter had, in an instant, planted himself in the line of escape. Merle put on speed, determined to make a go at just running the guy over. He had the momentum, but it never came to that, because from off to the right, the dancing lady in the pink gauze came twirling by like a Dervish and smashed into the waiter. The two of them went over like sacks of turnips. Merle leaped and cleared them. He streaked down the hallway, his steps making a racket. Out into the cool night, he ran for the cattails, shoving the photo in his jacket pocket and draping the camera belt around his neck.

It was dark but he managed to find the bike pretty quickly. As his ass hit the seat and he pedaled, he looked back over his shoulder. Shadowy figures emptied out through the lighted portal of the Thousand Eyes. When he reached the path a car started up behind him. His heart was pounding and the adrenalin was spurting out his ears. He pedaled with the belief that Ronnie Dunn's flunkies really meant to kill him. "Like Superman," Merle told Barney, "I was flying down that path, but I couldn't see a fuckin' thing. Behind me, I hear the car coming, and they're getting so close they've got me in their headlights."

In the midst of the chase, Merle reported having what he called "a moment of genius." He bet that with the confusion of the flash in the dark, no one could see he had an instant camera. He took it from around his neck and threw it back over his shoulder, hoping they'd at least stop to pick it up and that would buy him more of a lead. In fact, it worked. Not only did they stop, but once they had the camera they broke off their pursuit. Later, on the safety of Frog Road, heading toward Jericho, he realized he'd gotten away and could laugh at the thought of Ronnie Dunn holding the camera, discovering the shot Merle had taken was no longer inside it.

A lot was riding on that one photograph: the foundation to the grand finale of the Bars of South Jersey series. As he discovered, once back in his apartment, the door locked, that picture was a success in every way. It had that Polaroid-flash glare he'd come to love, sweeping vaguely down from the left corner. The hundred reflections of it off the glass behind the bar were like a distant constellation. Slow-dancing shadows with glowing red eyes. And Ronnie, eyes soulfully closed, with a corona of light around his head and bathed in white fire, his open mouth emitting a beacon of green mist. When he first saw it, Merle couldn't wait to get down to work, but as it turned out he put off starting the painting for nearly a year. He told Barney the photo had given him nightmares. And so the Bars of South Jersey series sat unfinished.

In September 1967, Hurricane Doria, only a Category 1, made it to the Jersey coast. It wasn't bad but for two tragedies it left in its wake. One made the national news; one made only the local radio station in Bridgeton. In the national news story, three people drowned when their boat sank off Ocean City. The local story, which Merle heard late at night while painting, was that the rising tide had swept away the Thousand Eyes. Upon hearing it he immediately went looking for the Polaroid from his visit there and found it under a stack of drawings. The bad dreams hadn't visited in months, and he laughed at his own foolishness, admonishing himself for not having already finished the series.

The same week the Thousand Eyes washed into the river and Merle started the painting, he peddled over to Milville for an art-show opening late one afternoon. He got there early and was standing on the sidewalk, waiting for things to get started. Last time he was there they had a tasty White Zinfandel. Across the street, in the shadow of the sub shop he noticed some commotion. Other people on the street were stopping and staring in that direction as well. It was the old couple from Jack's and the Eyes. The woman was pulling herself out of the grasp of the old man. She yelled, "I got to go. He's waiting." She'd move away from him a few feet and he'd run and catch her by the arm. "Don't go," he said. "Please, I can't stay," she said and pulled away again. "I'll go with you," he called. She didn't look back, and he didn't follow but leaned against the front of the sub shop and wiped his tears with a handkerchief.

Merle got blitzed that night at the opening, was shown the door, and could barely pedal home. Still he went back to work on the painting of the Thousand Eyes, putting everything he had into it. Two weeks later all that was left was Ronnie Dunn's weird left eyebrow, a couple of gray barnacles, and a small section of forehead. The rest was complete, perfect, capturing the Polaroid effects, the singer, and the grim, cold spirit of the lounge. Merle worked with a homemade, squirrel-hair brush to render the uptwist of the pale hair, concentrating so hard he perspired. As he executed the final stroke on the eyebrow, he heard something odd. Backing away from the painting, he reached behind him with his free hand and turned the radio down.

He listened, and eventually the soft noise came again. At first he mistook it for a mosquito, but then remembered it was the end of October. He closed his eyes and hearing it twice more recognized it as a distant voice. Someone calling out on the street, he thought. He laid the brush down, went to the window, and opened it. He stuck his head out, and above the sound of the wind, he heard the voice of Ronnie Dunn singing "Fond

Wanderer." He laughed, slammed shut the window, and went back to work, figuring someone in one of the buildings across the street was playing the old 45.

But as he painted on, the voice got louder and louder. As Merle told Barney, "It was like Dunn was out in the street, then in the downstairs foyer, then out in the hallway, then in the corner of the room. And the closer I got to finishing, the closer he got to me. I was shivering scared, but I was damned if I wasn't going to finish the series. I worked fast, without giving up anything in the quality, hoping that finally finishing would put Ronnie and the whole mess out of my misery." He finished the painting an hour later, "Fond Wanderer" booming in his head. The second he was done, he put on his jacket and headed for the door.

Merle said he knew what was happening, and the drive to follow the voice was monumental, like two metal fingers were hooked in each of his nostrils and attached by a chain to the *Queen Mary*, which was pulling out of port. He got as far as the door and opened it. And here's where my doubts about the story came in, because Merle attested to having another "moment of genius," and my credulity can only accommodate one Merle moment of genius per story. Barney convinced me, though, it all made sense. Anyway, Merle flung himself back into the room, grabbed the palette knife, and scraped off down to primer the last gray barnacle he painted on Ronnie Dunn's forehead. With that, the voice abruptly stopped, and he was no longer compelled to follow.

Two weeks later, he tried again to finish the series, and again the voice returned. He scraped it quick before Dunn got too loud. He found that as long as he left that swatch of canvas bare, the voice was silent. The kicker, as far as Barney was concerned, was that Merle eventually tried to get a show with the paintings of the bar series that were finished. He saved up and made slides and took them around to the different galleries. The gallery owners were intrigued by the local subject matter, but every one eventually passed, saying something along the lines of, "Really pretty good, but there's just something missing."

"And that," said Barney, "is the real voice of death."

Somewhere around 1975, Merle said he sold off for cheap, sometimes as low as twenty dollars, each of the paintings in the series, except for The Thousand Eyes. He confessed their presence was turning him into an alcoholic. As long as he had access to the last, unfinished piece, and could still complete it if he dared, it didn't matter to him where the other paintings were. Once the series was properly finished, it would take on a power greater than the sum of its parts, and Merle would, of course, be dead.

The painting of the Thousand Eyes hangs, as it has since 1976, above the booths in the back of Jack's Diner. Jack's son Dennis understands it's just for safekeeping. Barney said Merle swears that he's going to finish the piece any day now, but the old man does a lot more mumbling around town than painting lately, looking everywhere for that street that leads to The Land Where No One Dies.

Hibbler's Minions

It was 1933, and we wintered at the Dripping Springs west of Okmulgee. The Dust Bowl was raging, money was scarce. People didn't buy what they didn't need, but one thing they still needed was wonder. The folks out on the Great Plains could always scrape together a dime or two for Ichbon's Caravan of Splendors, a wandering menagerie of freaks and exotic beasts. We put on shows from Oklahoma to Ohio and back each year. Granted, the custom of carnivals was dying, and it faded another few inches with every town we rolled into. Dying wasn't dead, though, and in those days that was something.

Ichbon was an old-timer by then, having started out with Barnum in New York City at the American Museum when still in his teens. The great showman helped set the young assistant up with connections and cash to run the Caravan of Splendors. By the time I came to the Maestro, as we were required to call Ichbon, he had seen all the wonder he could stomach and at nights was given to drinking Old Overholt. Although he'd lost his sense of splendor, he retained his shrewdness for a dollar through those weary years and always managed to keep us in food, drink, and a little pocket money. He dressed like an admiral, complete with a cocked hat ever askew on his bald head. His trucks were dented, his trailers were splintered and rickety, his tent was threadbare, his banners were moth-eaten, and his beasts were starving. A lot of us, though, in the grasp of the Maestro, had nothing but the show between us and destitution. Who would hire a man born with an extra face on the back of his head? I was Janus, the Man Who Sees Past and Future. In reality, I saw neither, and even the present was murky.

On a day in late February, Ichbon instructed the laborers, also known in their act as the Three Miserable Clowns, to erect the tent so as to check it for repairs. In a few weeks we were due to set out on that year's journey. I was standing with him beneath the vaulted canvas, the ground still frozen beneath our feet, the sunlight showing dimly through the fabric. "What do you see in the future, Janus?" he asked me.

"Hopefully dinner," I replied.

"I predict a banner year for the caravan," he said.

"What makes you optimistic?"

"People are in such desperate straits, they'll seek refuge in nostalgia."

"Refuge we shall give them," I said.

"Nostalgia," said Ichbon, "is the syrup on the missing hotcakes."

Mirchland, the dwarf, appeared then through the tent's entrance with a stranger following. "Maestro," he said, "this is Mr. Arvet. He's come from all the way up by Black Mesa in the Panhandle to see you."

I could tell the man was a farmer by his overalls and boots, and that he was beset with hard times by the look in his eyes. His face was a dry streambed of wrinkles. Ichbon took off the admiral hat and bowed low. "A pleasure to meet you, sir," he said. He straightened and put his hand out to the man. "I am Ichbon." The Maestro's credo about the public was—"Treat them each like visiting emissaries from a venerable land. It's good for the cash box." The two shook hands. I expected the fellow to ask to join the show. I'd seen it before a hundred times. But instead he said, "I have something to sell you."

"What might that be?" asked Ichbon.

"It's out in my truck in a crate."

"An animal?"

"We had a black blizzard back in the fall. God's own wrath came barreling across the dead fields a mile high, and in its clouds it bore the face of Satan. You couldn't touch nobody in the midst of it or the electricity in the air would throw you apart. When it passed it left behind a plague of centipedes and a beast."

"Bring your truck in under the big top," said the Maestro, "and I'll have the clowns unload it."

Big Top, I thought, looking up at the tattered canvas, and my other face laughed.

I stopped laughing, though, when the Miserable Clowns, using all their strength, unloaded a long crate from the back of the truck. The sounds that issued forth from it reverberated inside the tent, reed thin but raspy, and their strangeness made my hair stand up. A moment later, a horrible stench engulfed us.

"Pungent," said Ichbon and drew out his handkerchief to cover his mouth and nose. From behind his makeshift mask, he asked Mr. Arvet, "Can you bring it out of the crate?"

"I made the box so the end slides open," said the farmer. "Do you have a cage of some sort we can empty it into?"

The Maestro gave orders for the clowns to bring the leopard cage, the leopard having given up the ghost through the harsh winter. The three buffoons brought the metal-barred enclosure and set it down so that its opening was congruent with the sliding panel of the crate. When all was ready, Mr. Arvet went to the box and pulled up the hatch. Immediately some large tawny-colored beast shot forth. It moved too quickly to see it well at first. The clowns dropped the sliding door of the metal cage and trapped it. Ichbon and I stepped closer to see.

"What in God's dry earth?" said the Maestro.

"Me and my woman call it the Dust Demon," said Arvet.

The Miserable Clowns backed out of the tent and fled.

The thing was as long as the leopard had been, but bulkier, more muscular, the very color of the grit that blew across the plains in those dirty days. Its body was covered with a fine, spiraled wool, and it moved on powerful legs, at the ends of which were paws with long, black, curving nails. There was no tail to speak of, just a stub, and the head was like nothing ever seen outside a nightmare. Its eyes were the tiniest black beads, and it had no ears, only holes that appeared as if they'd been drilled into either side of its skull. The mouth was wide, and there was no jaw, just a thin membrane in the shape of a giant open tulip, the whiskered edges rippling with life. The Demon grunted and then howled to discover it had not escaped. When its maw was wide, farther in there could be spotted rows of sharp black teeth.

"An abomination," I whispered from my other face, unable to help myself.

Arvet looked around as if unsure who'd spoken—he'd not seen my other me—and finally said, "Well, it is a demon."

Ichbon shook his head. "You say this came out of a dust storm?"

"Doc Thedus, up in Black Mesa, guessed it had been hibernating under the ground for centuries, and when the topsoil blowed away, it was awoken."

"Maybe," said the Maestro, "maybe." I could tell from his expression that he was seeing dollar signs. "How much do you want for it?"

"A hundred," said the farmer.

"A hundred dollars," said Ichbon and put the hat he'd been holding back on his head as if to make him think clearer. "No doubt you've uncovered a bona fide wonder here, Mr. Arvet. I'd like to make a deal with you, but I've not got a hundred to spare at this moment. We've yet to start this year's caravan. I'll tell you what I can do. I'll give you seventy dollars now, and in the fall, we can meet up in Shattuck, where we put on our last show, and I'll give you another fifty. That's more than you're asking. By then, we'll be flush after our journey to the east."

Arvet rubbed the back of his head and stared at the ground for a long time. "I suppose I could do that."

"Good enough," said the Maestro and shook hands with the farmer.

"What do we need to know about the Dust Demon? What does it eat? How do you care for it?"

"First off, you gotta be careful around it. The thing took down my neighbor's wife and ate her like a ham sandwich. Luckily he realized there was money to be made from it and instead of shooting it on the spot, helped me trap it. I gotta split the profits with him 70-30 of a hundred dollars. I guess I'll keep the extra twenty for myself."

"Besides farmer's wives, what does it eat?" I asked.

"Not sure," he said. "We had an outbreak of jackrabbits up there, and they were easy food to catch for it, so I fed it jackrabbits. It ate 'em but without any real enthusiasm. One thing's for sure, whatever you do, don't put any water near it. Water makes it weak. My wife put a bowl of water in its cage early on like you would do for a dog, and it almost perished on the spot till we come to understand it couldn't abide anything wet. Keep it covered in the rain."

That night, the Maestro gathered us beneath the tent and told us his plans for the Dust Demon and how the creature would save us all. Martina, the Dog Girl, described Ichbon's delivery as "grandiloquent," which all but Ichbon knew meant "meandering and tedious." The tent by then had trapped the Demon's stench, and we breathed it while the old man carried on. Finally, Jack

Sprat, the Thinnest Man Alive, said in a slightly raised voice, "It smells worse than shit in here." From its cage behind the speaker's podium the creature let loose a weak cry.

Ichbon took Sprat's cue and said, "In closing, I want to reiterate: the Demon will draw them, money will fill the coffers, and the Caravan of Splendors will rise from its economic hibernation to live again." We clapped once or twice, I wouldn't call it applause, and everyone made a beeline for the exit. Even the Maestro didn't stick around. He walked in a stately manner followed by the Three Miserable Clowns pantomiming him in the throes of his speech. They followed him, and I followed them, back to his trailer, where I knew the Old Overholt would flow. It seems that the Falling Angel and Maybell, the Rubber Lady, had the same notion as me. They were there, seated outside, passing the bottle with Ichbon when I arrived. A small fire burned in the center of their circle. There was an empty wooden folding chair, and I joined them.

The next morning, I woke in my trailer, with a headache from the whiskey and coughing out of both sides of my head from Maybell's harsh muggles. The only thing I could remember was the sight of Ichbon reeling drunkenly beneath the stars, going after the Three Miserable Clowns with a lion-taming whip. They were running around him, ducking and weaving, and he was snapping that thing in the air like gunshots. They were all laughing hysterically. "Miserable bastards," the Maestro bellowed and cracked the whip. When I left the trailer, hurrying to make it to breakfast on time, I nearly ran over Mirchland. He said, "The Maestro wants you in the tent in a hurry."

I was hungry, and the thought of facing the smell of the Dust Demon with a hangover didn't sit well. Still, I went. When I got there, I found Ichbon standing next to the cage of the creature. His hat was off, his head was bowed.

"Yes, Maestro," I said.

He nodded toward the cage. The beast was lying motionless. I stared for a long while, trying to notice the rise and fall of its breathing, but it was still. By that time, the flies had arrived, and although it seemed impossible the thing stunk worse.

"You see that on the floor of the cage?"

I nodded.

"That's the future."

"What are you going to do?"

"Considering I don't first blow my brains out and that I had the money, I'd have that thing stuffed," said Ichbon. "We could still make a fortune off the carcass with the right banner and bullshit in the towns, but a stitch job like that would sink us. I'm afraid we'll just have to move ahead without it." Never let it be said that the Maestro was a quitter. "The Dust Demon," he said as if picturing the creature rendered in full color bursting out of the ground toward an unsuspecting farmer's wife. Just then, I glimpsed a black dot of an insect leap off the creature's head and land on the back of Ichbon's wrist. He looked down, brought his hand closer to his eyes, and squinted.

Moments passed and he continued to study it.

"What is that?" I finally asked.

"It's a flea," he said. "Quick, go get the professor and round up the clowns." As I hurriedly left the tent, I saw, through the eyes in the back of my head, the Maestro cover the insect on his wrist with the opposite hand. He was smiling broadly. "When life is shit, make shit soup," he yelled after me.

Professor Dunce was Jon Hibbler's show name. He was the only one in the caravan older than Ichbon. Throughout his long life in the business he'd done nearly every act, once even passing as Jeez Louise, the Bearded, Tattooed Fat Lady. He'd seen all there was to see on the road, and the Maestro kept him around as a sort of advisor. Still, the creaky Hibbler had to pay his way and so pretended for the crowds that he was an imbecile. Dressed in a graduation gown and wearing a dunce cap, the professor would sit in a chair, and Ichbon would stand next to him, calling the patrons over and beseeching, "Ladies and gentlemen, could anyone really be this stupid?" It cost three cents to ask the dunce a question, and I never ceased to wonder how many couldn't wait to spend their pennies. Hibbler had a college degree, though, and had a rasher of high academic terminology that he would splice together to make a whirling lecture devoid of sense. The crowd loved their own love of his inanity.

The professor moved slowly, shuffling along amid the trailers in his black gown like some grim clergy. The cold affected him greatly. He was pale as a ghost, with a shock of white hair and a white beard. By the time I rounded up the clowns, Hibbler was just passing into the shade of the tent. Immediately, Ichbon ordered the clowns to go and bring back three glass jars with screw-on lids and eyebrow tweezers. Then he turned to the professor and said, "Do you remember, Jon, your act back twenty years ago, Hibbler's Minions?"

Ichbon's words took a moment to sink in, and then the professor smiled and said, "You mean the fleas?"

The Maestro stepped close to me and said, "This man, at one time, was the proprietor of the most renowned flea circus in the world. God, what a moneymaker it was."

"It was a good act," said the professor.

"What happened to it?" I asked.

"I couldn't get the fleas. You have to be able to loop a very thin gold wire around them to get them to perform. Cat and dog fleas are too small, but human fleas—*Pulex Irritans*—were large enough. I'd harness them to miniature chariots and have them walk a tightrope, carrying a little umbrella. At the end, I'd shoot one out of a cannon and catch it in midair. It's the cleanliness of the modern world that's put them in decline. You can't find them anymore."

The Maestro said, "I hope you still have some of that gold wire," uncapped his hand from off his wrist and brought it up for the professor to see more clearly. "Look at the size of that thing."

Hibbler nodded, slowly at first, but then with more determination. "I could work with that flea," he said. "It would be easy."

"I'll have the clowns collect as many as they can from the carcass of this worthless pile before I have it burned."

There came a day in early spring when the caravan finally lurched forward toward the rising sun. To be moving, to be caught up in a day's work, I found preferable to the purgatory of wintering. After the Dust Demon had been burned down to its bones and Ichbon had retrieved the skull and claws, the aroma lingered in camp till the day we departed. Despite the dust storms, everyone breathed easier on the plains, out of reach of the tentacles of that stench.

I brushed up on my act, which besides cheap tricks like inhaling a cigarette with one mouth and expelling the smoke out the other, took the form of an argument with myself. The Maestro always warned me, "Don't leave the audience for too long with your other face. It's too strange, too hungry. When it licks its lips, the customers walk away." I'd only viewed my other face once, in a room of mirrors, but the sight of me struck me unconscious on the spot. I was left with amnesia of the incident, unable to picture me. Whenever I tried, the hair would rise on the backs of my arms and the saliva would leave my mouth. I rewrote the script of the argument so that my other face had half as much dialogue. It meant fewer times I would have to turn completely around to answer myself, and that was fine with me as the act was exhausting.

The Maestro was right; the crowds that March were so dejected, they pretended we were good. By the time we made it to Muskogee, Professor Dunce had shed his graduation gown for a tuxedo and top hat and been reborn as Hibbler, Master of Minions. He sat with me and the Maestro and Maybell one evening. We passed the smoke and the bottle and he explained,

"These are no ordinary fleas. They're disproportionately large, with enormous heads. I can see their eyes watching for my commands. Under the jeweler's loupe I have discovered they don't have insect limbs, insignificant sticks, but muscular arms and legs with feet and hand-like grippers."

"But will they perform?" asked Ichbon, taking a toke.

"I dare say they're smarter than dogs," said Hibbler. "I don't even have to bind them and they willingly perform the feats I require."

"They feed on your blood?" asked the Rubber Lady.

"They don't touch me. When I doze off at night, they leave the trailer and go hunting. I think they must be into the animals, but I knew it was right to let them find their own diet. How much could they take? There are only six of them."

"The peacock is looking a little peaked," said Ichbon.

"When we open in Muskogee and you see the act and the money it brings, you won't care if they're feasting on your balls, Maestro."

"There's a lady present," said the face at the back of my head.

I saw the first show of the new flea circus, and Hibbler's Minions was the hit the old man had promised. Every night after the first, it was packed for his performance in the back left corner of the tent. The crowd could readily see the fleas and were astonished at what they'd been trained to do. Incredible lifting, pulling, acrobatics, tightrope walking, leaping, and all without a harness, all initiated by voice command from Hibbler. Laid out on a board was a three-ring circus, and in each ring a different flea performed a different feat. One lifted a silver cigarette lighter over its head, the next juggled caraway seeds, the third tumbled and leaped high into the air. Above them one crossed on a high wire. All six of them enacted a chariot race with two tiny chariots going around the circumference of the center ring. Word spread far and wide about the Minions. And when their act drew to a close the damn things would line up in a row and bow to applause.

Hibbler was back in old form and there was actually a spring in his step. He'd become the star attraction of the Caravan and was relishing it. "I rule them with an iron fist," he told me. "They know they'd better listen." But he dismissed me when I mentioned the fact that both the peacock and Brutus, the Orangutan, had recently passed on. Both animals were withered and lethargic in their final days.

"Do you really believe that fleas could drain an orangutan of its life? Please, Janus."

"There are only six," I admitted.

"There were only six," he said. "Now there are ten. But still, ten fleas?"

I lost my skepticism for a while in the success of the show. All the acts were doing well what with the crowd Hibbler drew. Instead of being pleased with the money that flowed in, though, the Maestro seemed anxious. Sometimes he didn't even wait for nightfall to start on the Old Overholt. "A tenuous thing, a flea," he was overheard to say. When the Falling Angel asked him what he meant, Ichbon whispered, "It's not the fleas I'm worried about in that act." Then the anteater was taken by an acute malaise and in a matter of a week became depleted and died. It was noted that the creature's eyes were missing at the discovery of its death. With this my skepticism returned, and I feared the Minions were behind it. Mirchland had the same idea, and we discussed it one night, standing under a full moon behind the mess wagon when neither of us could sleep for the phantom itching brought on by our knowledge of what was happening to the menagerie.

"All that's left is the albino skunk," he said. "Then what?"

By the next morning, the albino skunk had also gone the way of all splendors, and the caravan was for the first time since its inception without a menagerie of any sort, save fleas. The burial of the poor creature was pathetic. Everyone was there but no one had anything to say. Finally, Ichbon took his hat off, cleared his throat, and spoke. "I, for one, have no regrets seeing this overgrown rat pass on. It bit me once. In fact, I celebrate the passing of the entire menagerie. Good riddance to the damn beasts. The whole thing was a crime I'll now wash my hands of." When he was finished, the fleas dragged a dandelion onto the grave. Hibbler said, "Now say your prayers." I swear I saw them kneel all in a row and bow their heads. Mirchland looked up at me from the other side of the grave and carefully nodded. Beside me, I noticed the Falling Angel was looking pale, his once skintight lavender outfit now sagging with wrinkles.

Performers on the circuit agreed: the Falling Angel, Walter Hupsh, had an act so simple it was beautiful. He took a ladder to a platform at the peak of the big top, twenty feet in the air. Then he bent cautiously forward, grimaced, and fell. He was tall and lanky and not well built for it, plummeting like a bird forgetting its gift. Granted, there were two old mattresses buried in the packed dirt beneath the ladder where he hit. They were covered over with sawdust, and the public never knew. But still, with each performance there was an impact. Hupsh was head-rattled from a life of falling, that we knew, but a strange lethargy overtook him as we left Tulsa for Wichita. His trips up the ladder had become pathetic, his flights, as he called them, tragic. Mirchland and I kept tabs on him.

One afternoon, out of design, I sat next to him at lunch. "You look tired, Walter," I said. "Not been sleeping well?"

"I think I busted my ribs," he said, and a little drool of oatmeal issued from the corner of his lips. "And I got the itches something fierce. I wake up with the itches."

"Are you being bitten by a bug, maybe?" I asked.

"Yeah," he said and went back to his oatmeal.

In the days that followed, Walter came to rival Jack Sprat for most emaciated, and Sprat challenged the Falling Angel to a duel for sole ownership of the title. Cooler heads prevailed. The Maestro took me aside and said, "The falling guy looks like shit. Reminds me of the peacock."

I told him what I thought was going on and that Mirchland was on to it too. "Those fleas, whatever they are, drained the life out of all of the animals and now have turned to human blood."

"You mean Hupsh?" he said.

"Of course," I answered. "Look at him."

Just then the man was practicing his act. We looked over toward the center of the tent. The Angel took the ladder as if he were gravity itself. I could feel the weight of each labored step, but up he went, a trooper. Ichbon smoked a cigarette in the time it took him to reach the platform. Once there, he inched out to the edge. He stumbled, grasped at his throat, and groaned pitifully in the descent. He hit with a rattle. The Maestro and I ran to him. There was nothing left but a flesh bag of broken bones covered in sawdust.

When Ichbon caught his breath, he turned to me and said, "Get the clowns."

Mirchland and I were already there, sitting with Ichbon outside his trailer, passing the Old Overholt, when the Miserable Ones delivered Hibbler to our meeting. The Maestro said, "Pass the bottle to Jon," and I did. Hibbler was in his graduation gown, which, though no longer part of his act, he still wore to bed.

"We need to talk," said Ichbon.

"Give me a cigarette," said Hibbler.

I handed him one and he lit it with the silver lighter lifted by the flea in his show. His hands quivered. "Talk about what?" he asked.

"Falling Angel."

"A tragedy."

"We think your fleas did him in," said the Maestro.

"My fleas? You shouldn't have said that." Hibbler became indignant and sat up straight in his chair.

"They have to be squashed."

The old performer shook his head. "Impossible. There are too many of them. They're listening right now." The professor's bravado of recent weeks was gone, and he seemed shakier than he'd been since I'd known him. After a long draw on the bottle, he wiped his mouth, slumped forward, and gazed at the ground.

"I thought you were in charge," said Ichbon.

"I thought I was too."

"Let's burn them," said Mirchland in a whisper.

"No, you might as well set fire to yourselves and the whole damn caravan," said the professor. "Before you could light a torch they could be all over you, sucking you drier than no man's land."

"Well, I'm not going to sit around and wait till I'm on the menu," said Ichbon. "Call them together for a meeting and we'll ambush them."

"Shhh," said Hibbler. "I told you, they can hear us."

"Fuck the fleas!" yelled the Maestro.

Mirchland and I stood up and walked slowly away from the meeting.

Ichbon watched our dull escape. "You chickenshits," he said.

From my back mouth, I warned him, "Caution."

Two days later, the Maestro blew his brains out in his trailer. Jack Sprat found him, slumped back in his chair, a hole the size of a silver dollar between his eyes. There were also bullet holes in his feet, his shins, his stomach, his rear end, and his thigh. We knew he must have gone mad from the itching and tried to eradicate his persecutors with bullets. Only the Miserable Clowns dared to touch his corpse. They dragged it out to the edge of the field we were set up in, gathered brush, and made a bier. One by one, the members of the caravan came out of hiding to pay their last respects. There was less said at the event than for the burial of the albino skunk, but as his smoke rose, we watched with tears in our eyes, as much for our own fates as his. The Minions made a presence: their rank and file by the hundreds kneeled and prayed. When the fire burned down, the clowns retrieved the Maestro's blackened skull and mounted it on the bumper of the lead truck in the caravan.

Forgive me if I don't dwell on the list of my comrades who withered and succumbed to the hunger of the Minions. We left a trail of smoldering biers in our wake as we moved inexorably from town to town. By the time we hit St. Joseph, near the Kansas-Missouri border, Jack Sprat, Mr. Electric, the World's Ugliest Man and his beautiful wife, Ronnie, the Crab Boy, Gaston, the cook, and more had weakened, shriveled, and passed on. No one dared to speak about the horror we were trapped within. To speak out moved you immediately to the top of the menu. Whispers were dangerous. Those of us remaining had to take on more jobs in order to keep the caravan rolling.

Once the itching, started your hours were numbered. Most were dragged down in a state of grim and silent acceptance, but there were one or two who raged against it. The latter were far harder to witness, their antics pathetic against the inevitable. As for the performers who survived, the stress of insect servitude, the fact that they were like cattle kept for slaughter, quickly began to undermine their acts. The fortune-teller saw only one future. The knife-thrower's hands fluttered like trapped birds, and his poor assistant was numb with the fear that if the fleas didn't kill her he would. The Miserable Clowns lost their sense of humor. As terrible as the rest of the caravan was, at each stop the crowd still showed up to see Hibbler's Minions. The new grand finale of the act consisted of thousands of fleas coming together to form the figure of a man tipping his flea hat to the audience.

Mirchland and I, cautiously passing written notes, planned our escape. We were fairly certain the fleas could not read. St. Joseph was to be the spot where we would take our leave of the caravan. The plan was to disappear with the crowd at the end of Hibbler's act, to mingle in with them and, once to the road, try to hitch a ride or run for it. Not much of a plan, but we were desperate. The correspondence we had going was voluminous, most of it pondering the fact that the fleas obviously intended to drain all of us in the carnival before dispersing out into the general population. We never saw news of flea infestations from the towns we passed through and wondered why the Minions didn't spread out and share their horror with the rest of the world. Mirchland thought it was because they were building strength, increasing their numbers for an all-out assault on some unsuspecting hamlet in our path. I, on the other hand, thought it had to do with that part of their act where they transformed through accretion into the figure of a man. "Only together can they achieve their terrifying potential," I wrote to the dwarf.

Just as we planned, when the evening show let out on our second night in St. Joseph, I met my friend behind the clowns' trailer. He'd packed a small satchel he had attached to a stick and had a lantern in his hand, the wick brought down so as to only offer a mere glow. He was sitting on an overturned milk crate, his back against the trailer wheel, his feet off the ground. "Hurry," I said to him. "Let's go." I was anxious to be on the move. As I stepped away from him, my other me noticed that he didn't budge. Then I spotted his empty eye sockets, and spun around.

The fleas issued forth from the twin puckered holes where his eyes had been, two living streams of black. Single file, and if my ears did not deceive me, singing some kind of song in unison. I gagged, doubled up with fear, and fell on my knees. The fleas marched along the ground to within two feet of me and then drew together to form the word "sorry" in my very own script. Something bit my rear end, a warning that I'd not be going anywhere. To my surprise, they didn't infest me. I supposed I was to be saved for a later meal. Returning to my trailer in a stupor, I spent the night scratching my ass, the itching from just that one bite an agony. The prospect of inevitably being overrun with them made me consider Ichbon's method of scratching with a revolver no longer insane.

Granted, the fleas were shrewd, but the next day, after torching Mirchland's remains, the caravan headed away from Missouri and back toward the heart of Kansas. Everyone who had been with the show for a couple of years knew this was wrong, but no one mentioned it. I surmised immediately what was going on. The Miserable Clowns, who drove the trucks that pulled the trailers, were taking us out into the plains, away from the towns and cities. To be honest, I was shocked that they'd have the foresight or concern. When the fleas got through with us, there was nothing stopping them from overrunning humanity. The plan, as I perceived it, was to strand us out in the heart of the Dust Bowl and let them eat each other after they'd devoured us. In the end, if the world was to be saved, it would be saved by miserable clowns.

For the next three days straight, the caravan rolled at top speed, at first on a road, passing small dilapidated farms and one-horse towns, and then on a packed-dirt path that cut through the sandy remains of what had once been pasture. The sky was blue, but you'd hardly know it as the dust blew up around everything, choking the air and blocking the sun. Myself and I had to wear kerchiefs around our mouths and noses and something to protect the eyes from the blowing grit. I opted for goggles and my other me settled for an old wide-brimmed hat pulled low. The hours dragged tediously on as we passed through the desolation. Late on the third afternoon, when the caravan came to a halt somewhere in the far-flung dry heart of America, the clowns were informed by Hibbler that there would be no more driving. The fleas needed to perform.

The trailers were gathered into a half circle as the night came on and then lit by lanterns and torches. There was no paying public for a hundred miles in any direction. We performers were to be the audience. There wasn't any choice. We gathered on folding chairs, forming a half circle around Hibbler and a small, makeshift stage for the fleas. The old man wore his graduation gown instead of his tuxedo and top hat. He stood before us, weaving to and fro, with an insipid smile on his face. When the crowd quieted down, he lifted the graduation robe over his head and dropped it on the ground. One more horror to add to the onslaught: a completely naked Hibbler stood before us.

There were audible groans from the crowd and someone in a most pitiful voice whispered, "No more." As if those words were the cue, the old man's entire body was covered instantly by fleas. It happened so fast, I thought it was a trick of shadows from the torchlight. But no, every inch of him, instantly. His screams were muffled by the Minions filling his mouth. They remained latched to Hibbler, pulsating en masse with the rhythm of feeding. And then as quickly, they were gone. His corpse remained standing for a moment—snow white, shriveled, sucked dry—before collapsing in upon itself. We gasped and rose to our feet, standing there stunned, wondering what would come next. It took no more than a moment for us to realize—this was to be the end of the road for Ichbon's Caravan of Splendors. The fleas had somehow detected the unspoken treachery against them.

They struck again, covering in an eyeblink the slouching form of Hector, the Geek, making a mummy of him in less time then it took him to bite off a chicken head. As he fell away, they settled on the juggler and his apprentice. The Three Miserable Clowns stepped forward then, brandishing jars full of gasoline. They doused the writhing, flea-draped forms, and then the most miserable of them all flicked his lit cigarette at them. The sudden explosion knocked me off my feet. The next thing I knew, I was helping me up and we were running away from the caravan into the night. Ahead it was pitch black, and behind I saw flames engulfing the trailers, bodies strewn on the ground, and a man's form made of fleas, tipping his hat to me and waving.

I ran at top speed like I never had nor ever would again, and when I finally stopped to catch my breath, at least a mile from the burning caravan, my other me admonished me. "Up you laggard," he bellowed. "They can suck you dry, but I want to live. Get moving." I pulled myself together and took off again. I wandered over dunes and across barren fields. When the wind finally died down and the sky cleared enough to let the moonlight through, I found an abandoned house, one whole side up to the roof covered in sand. Smaller dunes surrounded the entrance. Exhausted, I pried open the door, pushing a foot of sand away. Inside, there were two rooms. One was full to the ceiling with sand. The other was clear and had a rocking chair by a window that still offered a partial view of moonlight on the waste.

The next day, I awoke in the rocker to the roar of a black blizzard moving across the prairie. The approaching sound, like a locomotive, woke me. I ran outside to see it coming in the distance. Dust two miles high, rolling toward me, a massive brown cloud one might mistake for a mountain range. I'd survived the caravan and now I was to be buried alive. I told myself I would stand my ground, but the sand that was pushed ahead of it in the wind stung me everywhere, and I thought of fleas biting me. Before I turned and ran for the house, I saw it as Arvet had described: the face of Satan coalescing in the roiling dust—horns and snake eyes and maw open, hungry as a flea. I got inside and shut the door behind me just when it hit. Huddling in the corner of the clear room, I took off my jacket and threw it over my faces. The air grew thick with dust, and the noise outside was deafening.

That night, after Satan had passed, I dug out. On my march back to civilization the following morning, I came upon the carnival half buried in sand and tumbleweeds. I saw the drained corpses of my colleagues, even those of the Three Miserable Clowns. No sign of the fleas, though, as if the dust storm had sent them back into hibernation. I broke into Hibbler's trailer and took the cash from the cash box—considerable given the success of the flea shows. I managed to get one of the trucks going and drove down to Liberal, Kansas, where I eventually settled. I was surprised folks there accepted me for what I was, but then my having two faces was the least of their problems in those years.

I never spoke about the fate of the caravan, yet I often pictured it out there on the plain, covered over with blowing sand. A couple years later, I was volunteering for the Red Cross in one of their makeshift hospitals, treating those laid low by the dust plague, when I came upon a female patient brought in after a blizzard, close to death's door. It was Maybell, the Rubber Lady. She was in a bad way, wheezing up clouds of dust, her chest rattling like a hamper of broken china. She remembered, called me Janus and smiled. In the evenings, when the ward was quiet, I sat by her bedside and we reminisced about the show and Ichbon and the appearance of the Minions. She told me she'd escaped being drained because her flesh was too elastic. That got me thinking and I said to her, "That's the one thing I always wanted to know. Why they allowed me to escape."

"I know," said Maybell, barely able to speak. She motioned for me to draw closer, and I leaned in. "Hibbler told me it was that face on the back of your head. They felt some kind of kinship for it."

I wasn't sure whether to thank her for that, but my other me did.

Monster Eight

I ran into the local monster a couple of times behind the laundromat on my way home with clean clothes. He had a base of operations back there since it was only a short dash into the woods behind the place. That forest goes on for a hundred miles. I don't know what he's a monster of; everybody said he was definitely one, but I hadn't seen it. He was just a fat guy who sat at a desk made of a plank and blue plastic milk crates. He had a hot orange scoop chair with three legs that he balanced on. For my money, he was just a sad sack. He was always looking at the woods over his shoulder, seeming to contemplate dashing back into them at the drop of a hat. A hairy motherfucker, though. You could stuff a mattress with just the crop off his back. And his conversation was self-deprecating but not in a humorous way. He was always apologizing for everything—the weather, his mood, the news of the day. A monster of sorry, I'd give him that.

So after having said hello to him when leaving the laundromat a few times, one day I stopped and asked him why he was sitting back there in a parking lot no one ever ventured into, save a drunk, looking for a place to piss, maybe a curious kid on a bike every blue moon, or me heading home from the laundromat on the path through the woods. He seemed surprised that I spoke to him. His eyes widened, raising his brows, and deep flesh moved around the horns protruding from his temples. Granted, the horn thing was a turnoff. Like what am I talking to? A buffalo? It's not a good look if you want to be taken seriously. So I had to get past that. I swallowed hard and waited for my answer. He grunted a little and I could tell he was nervous. His leg shook and it rattled the desk plank.

"I've got business back here," he said.

"What's your business?"

"I do my monster thing."

"Who pays you? Who's gonna pay to get harassed by a monster?"

"I'm a pro bono monster."

"Working for the good of the people?"

"That's right. I want to create an epic experience for everyone."

"How do you do that?"

"Get into their lives, and then I see what the biggest problem they have is, and I turn up the monster bs level to just above that. They battle the monster and survive and then their real problems don't seem that difficult. That's the gist."

"What's monster bs?"

"Could be everything from some light haunting, calling out their name in a spooky voice in the middle of the night, to shooting right up their toilet and taking a bite out of their ass. It's all in a day's work."

"Sounds rewarding. I heard you bit the head off the Miller girl. What was she? Sixteen? Some collateral damage?"

"That's not true. She's in town right now, still tweaking. The kid's got nine lives. People tell all kinds of stories about me."

"My problem with the whole charade is that you're not scary in the least," I said.

"There's scary and there's scary."

"Right, and you're not either one of them." I got kind of a thrill from telling off the local monster. Not wanting that feeling to fade, I added, "You're more pathetic than anything else."

"OK, OK, I can see where this is headed," he said. He stood up to his full height. He was tall, maybe eight feet, and wide with rippling muscles beneath the red sleeveless T and hair and fat.

My obstreperousness wrinkled away in the shadow of his stature. He came around the desk and put an arm across my shoulders.

"What are you doing?" I asked.

"Look, there's no longer any reason for me to go on with this. You see through me. But, since you're not afraid of me, you wouldn't mind taking a walk in the woods."

"Where to and why?"

"I may not be mythic but I've got something mythic to show you."

"Well, I have to go through the woods anyway. What do you say you stop at my place so I can drop my laundry off? Then we'll check out whatever it is you've got going."

"OK," he said and led the way toward the boundary between the parking lot and the woods. I caught up with him and as we crossed over, I heard him breathe a sigh of relief. We got on the path and headed northwest where it would eventually lead to my place out in the sticks on the edge of farmland. Side by side, we ambled onward at a long slow gait. He complained about how out of shape he was, apologized for it, of course. I asked him if he could at least give me a hint as to what he would show me later. He stopped for a moment on the trail, paws on hips. Looking into the sky, he shook his head. "All I can tell ya is it's connected to the ideas of fulfillment and the growth of the spirit."

"That sounds like monster bs," I said.

"For real. That's what it's about. I'm taking a chance showing this to you."

"Calm down," I said.

The woods became a forest, the canopy thicker and blocking more light. There were spots where sun came down like a transporter beam from *Star Trek* and puddled on the path, but there were shadows too, and they were extra cold. Somewhere along the line, his complaints about himself turned into a story he spoke in cadence with our steps. Occasionally, purple finches darted above us. The trees grew taller as we went along, the oaks and pines like columns and spires in an enormous cathedral.

"I remember some real monsters," he said. "For instance, my uncle, Ted. He was old school, tear 'em up, pop off a head, no reason needed. You know, just a total hard-ass. And he looked terrible, lumps all over him, a pig nose, nails that were claws, pointed teeth, a fucked-up face. He'd show up at a party with a pair of long knives and leave the place looking like a bad night at Benihana's. *Slaughter* was his nickname among his friends. He ran with a crowd of other monsters who called themselves the Magnificent Seven. Seven monsters all impressively horrible. Each of them had a special trait and each a nickname. There was Bite 'Em, who bit people a hundred times in a minute, and one with the name Shit Breath Academy. He just opened his mouth and reality wilted. You get the picture. Seven monsters with more monster bs than you could shake a stick at. They were full of themselves, taking liberties with their mythic power, not to mention murder and mayhem in tall order. As they achieved the height of their power, there appeared on the scene a new kind of monster. He went by the title Monster Eight. And he let it be known that he had come to defeat the Magnificent Seven.

"Monster Eight was different, more reptilian, and had the ability to morph into any human form he had ever seen. His feet were molded in the form of high heels, his flesh was pebbled in red scales. He could leap, run fast, and was strong, but his most dangerous asset was his voice and what it said. In the end Monster Eight shut them all down, one through seven. Talked them right out of their lives. Uncle Ted split his own head with a hatchet. It took Monster Eight seven minutes to convince the old dope he was better off away in the cosmic elsewhere. Once his task was complete, and the seven were gone, he disappeared. No one knows where he went. It's said that he wanders the world, unable to die until eight centuries have passed."

I wanted to hear more, but we were approaching my house. Lynn was on the porch in her rocker. I waved as we came out of the woods and walked across the field. I could see her stand up and go inside. The moment I saw it, I knew exactly what was going on. She went inside to get her father's pistol. She knew immediately that I was walking with the local monster. As we reached the porch, I started up the steps, but she pushed through the screen door with the gun out in front of her aiming at my new associate. "Stay there," she said to me. "And you," she said to the monster, "you make a move and I'll drill you with all six."

"Have no fear, madam," said the monster and put his paws up.

Lynn pointed her gun at me. She said, "Give me the laundry." She reached down the step and I reached up. She took the stack by lacing a single finger under the knot of twine at the top of the package. In her opposite hand the gun wobbled and made me nervous. Once she had the laundry she said, "I'm gonna give you about two minutes to get that fucking thing out of here. Then I'm just gonna start shooting. You come home with the local monster? You're out of your mind. Early onset, if you know what I mean. I can't believe I've put up with 40 years of your stupid shit."

"He's got mythic qualities," I told her. The monster nodded without lowering his arms.

"He smells like an epic shit. I can't believe you can stand the smell of him. Move it along." She looked directly at me and then her gaze went slowly out across the field toward the old white garage and she winked. "Unload this walking turd and get back here for dinner. Hurry up."

I turned to the monster and apologized for my wife calling him a walking turd. He shrugged and said, "Not uncalled for by any means."

We stood out front for a few minutes, and I made as if I was unsure if I wanted to take the journey. When he started to get impatient, reminding me I had promised to go, I said, "Come to the garage with me. I have an ATV in there that we can take out into the woods. We'll go see your deal and then I can get home quick."

"I do have an appointment to break a priest's legs this evening, so if we could pick up the pace, that would be fine," he said.

We headed for the garage, a big building at the edge of the field beneath a white oak. I let him lead the way. "Your wife is lovely," he said. I quietly laughed. He opened the whitewashed door and stepped into the dark. "Hey, where's the light switch?" he asked. An instant later I heard him get wacked by whatever she wacked him with. I guessed it was that big plumber's wrench just by a twinge of a metallic ding as it cracked his skull. He went down like an eight-foot furry sirloin and slapped the cement floor. We worked together and had him strung up in chains in no time. In the middle of the garage there was a large hole dug through the concrete and fifteen feet into the ground. Lynn emptied a can of lighter fluid into the hole. We shared a cig, discussing the clean, accurate blow to his head. Before the smoke was out, I tossed it into the pit. The flames took and in no time he was awake and in agony at the melting of his flesh. The screams kept up for a while. The whole thing really stunk.

Right when we thought he was finished, and things simmered down to a sizzle and an occasional pop, Lynn called me over to the rim of the pit. She had been inspecting the remains from above with a powerful flashlight. I joined her at the edge and she said, "What's happening?" I squinted and could see in the harsh beam that the charcoal remains of the local monster were splitting open. "We've done three of them so far, and none of them before has done this after roasting for forty-five minutes," I said.

"Yeah, this ain't right."

"Do you have the gun?" I asked.

She pulled it out of her pocket, and as she did, the remains of the local monster, a flame-blackened shell, split open, and something quick as a wink shot out and hovered up by the rafters. It was red, with a long, flickering tongue.

"Oh shit," I said. "It's Monster Eight."

"No."

"Plug it," I yelled. She fired, and her shot went wide through the roof. I grabbed her arm as we made for the door of the garage. It chased us out across the field toward the house. Lynn stopped twice in our escape and each time fired a shot at it. It seemed she hit it twice, as it was bounced back through the sky a few yards with the impact of each bullet. We ducked into the house, ran upstairs to our small library, and shut the door. I pulled the copy of *The Marble Dance* in the first bookcase to our right, and the shelves opened like a door. We ducked and stepped into the darkness, and the bookcase closed behind us. In that cramped space, we held each other. Only once we were in there did it become clear that we should have left the gun outside. We heard him enter the room and heard him draw a chair up next to the shelves we were behind. The flow of his reasoning was such that I was already convinced about early inconsequential points in an argument for suicide before I realized he was speaking at all. His bleak message was relentless. We each closed our eyes, drew nearer, and staked our love against his monstrous powers.

Inn of the Dreaming Dog

Start in a car and drive due west till your money for gas runs out or the vehicle fails, shedding parts, coughing, jerking to a standstill, hissing steam into the blue. Then you can hire a guide to take you on foot over the snowcapped purple mountains. The peaks are so tall and so treacherous and teeming with creatures who feast upon weary travelers.

In the past there were a number of guides to choose from, and the price wasn't too dear, but the mountain eventually took all their lives but one. The one that remains, a brooding fellow known as the Misanthrope, is the most accomplished guide of any who has ever traversed the treacherous way. But now he tells his customers, "This may be my last trip." They ask if he is planning to retire, and he scowls and says, "No, die!" The customer finds this frightful news and says, "What'll happen to me if you pass away on the mountain?" "Should I care?" roars the Misanthrope.

Then the customer gets a good look at their guide and sees that Gaspar Maloney, master navigator through the purple mountains, is so old that a big patch of skin on the left side of his face has turned to leather, his hair to straw, and his eyes are cracked and yellowed as ancient ivory. When he speaks, a black sand like pepper blows out of his mouth, the disintegrating detritus of his weakest organ, the heart.

Gas, as all know him, of course, charges a higher price once he becomes the sole guide. It isn't money he wants, though. He never goes to town, buys almost nothing, but resides in a cabin at the base of the mountains, living off the bounty of the land. What he asks in payment is the customer's pinky finger. The price really doesn't make any sense. If money is useless to him, what good is a cut-off pinky finger going to be? For certain, people try to argue him out of it by offering a horse, a pistol, a lifetime supply of steaks. Nothing makes a difference. If you want to have as good a chance as you can get in arriving alive at the Inn of the Dreaming Dog, you have to resign yourself to one less finger.

All payment is up front. Gas's method for removing the digit involves a rusty pair of garden clippers. The ritual takes place inside the hollowed-out trunk of an enormous tree, whose branches tear at the clouds and rings lead back to the origin of everything. Just before reaching for the clippers, Gas lights a big fat cigar of rolled foxglove petals. He puffs it up and gets it smoking with a red-hot ash. The patient gets an old piece of boot sole to bite on. Then snip, crunch, a spurt of blood, and the sad little appendage falls into a bucket of chopped-off fingers. Gas grabs the throbbing wrist and lifts your arm. With his free hand, he jams the end of the cigar onto the fresh wound and seals it with a sizzle.

What this whole bizarre operation points to is just how badly those who are traveling want to reach the inn. And so, the next morning, with a phantom finger screaming in agony, you set out, following Gas up through the yellow leaves of the birch stands on the eastern side of the mountain. One is right to wonder why such a treacherous journey is undertaken in late autumn. Winter must play a part. When asked about the season, Gas, if he answers at all, says, "The cold is cleanly." The ascent is steep, but the guide knows a secret path that takes his party inside the mountain. There they find steps and a handrail carved from the very rock. All along the interior passage are ancient paintings of fantastic beasts and men in bird masks.

Ask Gas Maloney the meaning of any of it and he'll reply,

"From the dawn of time there's been no shortage of ways that folks have found to waste their precious hours." Still, to the untrained, unaccustomed eye, the work of the bygone artists is beautiful, one surprise after another. In the torchlight, the colorful forms appear to move. Certain travelers attest to the fact that they most definitely heard the sounds of breathing all around them, and when bedding down at night on one of the occasional landings among the seemingly infinite steps, they were awoken by far-off echoing screams. It could all have been in the mind, but then why would a startled traveler, torn from sleep, open their eyes on a scene of Gas, shivering, holding a lit torch, his pistol at the ready?

Another day in the darkness, climbing the throat of the mountain, and they reach the mouth, so to speak, and are regurgitated out somewhere above the tree line. The winds are brutal there, the sky, nothing but blue. And the snow is hip deep at least. This is where if someone on the journey, a husband or wife or partner, any member of a party, is holding up the progress of said pilgrims, Gas makes sure they meet with a fatal accident. Usually a fall into the spiral ice crater it takes a day to hike around. If the remaining members of the party grouse about it, he gets in their faces and yells, "Shut yer pie hole." If you don't, an ice pick to the forehead is his strategy.

On his journeys back and forth from his cabin to the inn, he often passes the remains of his victims. His justification is, "If you can't cut it, you don't deserve to visit the inn." The words spill over his blistered lips. The way he escapes prosecution is that those who plan to visit the inn have no intention of ever returning. So, whether they are enjoying the sublime stillness of Willow Pond or rotting at the bottom of an ice fissure, it's all the same to the outside world. Though he hates them all equally, Gas is committed to getting those who can withstand the rigors of the journey to their destination and has safely delivered far more than he has extemporaneously dispatched.

And just think, say you actually happen to be on Gas's last trek. It's you and the old guide, and you've made it to the downhill winter slope that leads to the valley of the inn, and right there in the thinning snow of your descent, he goes over hard like five sacks of potatoes off the back of a truck, dead before he hits the ground. What will you do? You might try to go back, but even in your frightened state you know that will be certain death. Besides, you've promised your wife or husband or partner that you would meet up at the Inn of the Dreaming Dog. You might fall into despair, but instinctively you know what's at the end of that trail. No, I imagine you'll frantically pull yourself together and continue on. But first, will you bury Gaspar Maloney? Or leave him to the wolves and snow rats? Bury him?

No, of course not. You've never let on, let him see it or feel it, but you've despised him every step of the way. You feared for the entire journey to close your eyes at night at the thought of what he might do to you. The thing foremost on your mind is that leather patch of his face—cracked, rough, the colors of reptiles—you pray, and you're not particularly religious, that you might never have to touch it for eternity. In fact, you flee the Misanthrope's corpse for fear he might find a trail back to life. Just admit it and let's move on. Down you go, all the way down.

Just past the tree line, having finally left the snow behind, you can see the lush green of the valley below, smell its bouquet of pine, mountain laurel, flowering dogwood, and snapdragon. As you descend, you hurry, anxious to see your loved one, anxious to be not alone anymore, but your hurry makes you lose your step and you pitch forward into a roll and slide and bounce down the mountain. A mile or more you careen, getting the stuffing knocked out of you, and are finally abruptly stopped by the massive trunk of a cedar.

From then on, realizing yourself lucky not to be dead, you rise and stagger forward. There are no stores left in your pack by then. You're thirsty when you finally discover the dirt road that leads to the inn. Or at least you hope it leads to the inn. Somewhere around midnight, about to fall down from exhaustion, you use your last match in order to read the words on the first sign post you've come to. There is an arrow pointing down the road and the words *Inn of the Dreaming Dog* are sloppily carved.

The next day after rising, you may find wild blueberries along the side of the road or if you still have enough energy left you might hunt down a squirrel with your ice axe, given you've kept it until this point and not tossed it to lighten your load. But let's not forget the time it will take for you to have skinned it. Too much time. You'll be wanting to get to the inn before sundown. You're Achilles tendon is aching from your having run in your dreams, chased by a fierce dog. In the bright morning light, you notice the full skeletons along the sides of the dirt path. Sun-bleached skeletons, ever pointing toward the destination they will never achieve. Take them as a sign, each a kind of monument to failure, and push on through the pain.

Here is where you remember your loved one. By now you know they are waiting for you in the leisure of the garden patio, listening to the charming artist from Rome spinning a mournful story about an individual's affair with a ghost. They are waiting for you deep in the surrounding forest, along the creek, where the ruins of an old graveyard have been swallowed by the trees. The wind is in the leaves, and there's a chill in the air. They are waiting for you at night, on the porch, in a creaking rocker, half drunk on wine and staring at the moon. The night erupts with the sound of breathing and a distant cry.

There is a proper sign, neatly lettered at the end of the drive that leads away from the dirt road. The path to the big house is paved with round white stones. Flowers have been planted all along the walk, mostly roses red and yellow, some daisies, cosmos, and sunflowers. You 'll look up, of course you will, to see the place. A three-story wonder of a house with gingerbread trim, a wraparound porch, a large cupola in the center of the top floor with doors that open to a third-story porch. The place stands solidly like it has been and will be there forever. The color is a sea-foam green with white trim. It looks brand-new but how can that be? From the porch to the screen door to the lobby, and when you enter the lobby, all tension, all pain, drain out of you.

The proprietress, who is always at the ready to welcome new guests, syphons off your cares and lets them pour into a big mason jar that one is given as an initial token of hospitality. Do what you like with it, pour it out, hide it under your bed. It's been said that only by drinking that poison swill might you have a chance of returning to the world. Since the beginning of the inn, no one has made it past the nauseating smell of the mix in order to so much as take a taste. The aroma is said to contain the stench of every dark moment of your life, even the secret ones. Besides, the inn is cool and calm and wonderful. A bucolic daydream, like a place from the center of your wish lobe. Why would you want to leave?

The proprietress, Miss Sally (some of her longtime guests call her Sally Forth, as she has never married but has constant secret affairs with her boarders; her name is Alice Sally), takes you gently by the arm and gives you a tour of the inn and its gardens and ponds and walkways and gazebos. One room is taken up by a giant fish tank holding brightly colored tropical fish, a human skull the size of three, and an octopus that lives behind the eye holes as the very brain of it. The library is massive—on that first day, you never make it to the end of the stacks—and everywhere you look you see volumes you've never heard of by your favorite writers. You visit the parlor, where couples play cards and two ladies smoke cigarettes and quietly whisper about the gentleman across the room dozing over his volume of *The New Adventures of Maqroll.*

The room contains a gorgeous chandelier, each of its crystals a beacon of enchantment. Around the corner at the back of the oasis is a short dark hall that leads to a snooker table. And there beneath the glow of a dim bulb Manfred Jenkins and Shell Tock discuss in whispers neither you nor Alice Sally can hear a plan to escape the Dreaming Dog. You are shown one calm, contemplative room after another—the dining hall and its 100-yard table, the grotto, directly below the library, accessible by a secret door and winding bone stairway, lit only by blind, phosphorescent fish in a warm underground pond, the den of the Dog's masseuse, the crystal tea room, made entirely of glass and overlooking the inn's vegetable gardens. And finally, not a room too soon, your room.

The feather down mattress of your bed rests on the cherrywood hand-carved likeness of a sea turtle. The proprietress promises that after the sun has left the sky, and its effluvium no longer seeps in your windows, the floor of your room will glow blue and the ceiling will appear a dark sky full of stars. On the small table next to your bed there is a pitcher of water, a plate of sliced lotus, and a pipe full of the inn's special blend of hashish, orange peel, and violet petals known as Pistol Witch. You are shown the rope you are to pull for room service and told that dinner is at six sharp. You are warned not to miss it. Alice Sally smiles but says, "The consequences are severe for those who are tardy or absent." Wanting to seem compliant, you nod eagerly and then see you have put off your hostess by too great a display of acquiescence.

She turns to leave you to your new life, but you call out, "Just one thing." She stops, her back to you, and does not move. You say, "I'm looking for my partner," and you give their name and inquire as to their room number. The proprietress is silent for a moment, but as she exits your room, you hear her laughter. It trails away down the hallway. Something seems off to you about the inn. You push it out of your head. You know you need to freshen up, change your clothes, and set out quickly to locate your love.

All this is accomplished in a thrice; you mark the location and number of your room, so as not to lose yourself to the Dreaming Dog, and push off into Eden. You've managed to smuggle through from the other side of the mountain a photo of your partner. You hid it under a liner in your boot, and you got Gas drunk the night he inspected your gear for illegal contraband. It's illegal to take any kind of picture or book to the other side. There are those who've been killed for it and one or two sent back, which was supposedly far worse. In any event, you have the picture and are dead set on using it. You start at the Cocktail Lounge on the southern terrace.

The very first person you try happens to be Manfred Jenkins, direct from his conspiratorial rendezvous at the snooker table. He grumbles to you, "You know, a photo like that, from the other side, will get you in trouble here. Throw it away and forget about it." He doesn't walk away after speaking, though, but continues to stare at you. Yes, he has prodigious sideburns. Yes, his face is an ass, gray in complexion. As you move to show the photo to someone else, he grabs you by the collar and pulls you close. His breath is rutabagas and shit. He whispers and this time you do hear him. "You look like a real malcontent," he says. "Like you've seen to the core of this chicanery and you're ready to bust out. Would you agree?" He releases you and you instinctively take a step back. You nod and give him as much of a yes as you can muster through your fear.

"Tonight," he says, "me and my partner, Shell, and the masseuse, we're going over the garden wall, so to speak. Heading on, further in, to the Source of Glory." "What's that?" you ask. "The next inn down the road," he says. "I've heard you don't have to be on time to meals, you can sleep as much as you want, cheap beer night, Bingo, you know, better shit." "Can you get weed there?" you ask. Manfred giggles. He assures you that is not a problem at the Source. Then he leans over and speaks like a distant cry into your ear. "Through the library through the secret door, to the Grotto. Dive in, dive deep, and let the blind fish guide you with their lights. You will come up in a pool on the other side of the inn's boundaries. The Dog will have no hold on you. And, by the way, your partner, I just saw them before coming in here a moment ago, out on one of the divans in the Mushroom Garden, reading a book."

You thank Manfred profusely and then you're off, asking along the way for directions to the spot. You are sent outdoors and off to the east and then south through the ostrich stables, around the Fountain of the Demon Fairy to look for a path through the woods that will lead to where the mushrooms grow. As you are frantically jogging, it strikes you that the sky is darkening. You look at your watch—5:50 p.m. Dinner will be served imminently and you need to be there, but you must see your partner. After all these years, first you will find them and then you can flee to the dining hall holding hands, together again. But now you've made a turn around the corner of a wooden corn crib, expecting to see the path to the Mushroom Garden. There are three paths leading into the woods. You stop to think which one you should take, and a few moments later wake from a daze, already walking along a path in the woods.

The sun is setting and the thickets are filling with indigo and stars. An owl calls. The wind blows strong against you on the path. Time sidles by and is gone on ahead. At exactly 6:01 p.m., you look up, drawn by the sound of someone crying in the distance. There on a white divan on the side of the path, is your partner, your friend. You rush to them. Their eyes are dark and glassy, and in their hand, you find the Pistol Witch pipe. They wake suddenly and see it is you, and they cry, and you cry, wrap your arms around each other and hold tight. A comet passes overhead with a golden tail and drops sparks down through the trees. You kiss.

Your partner pulls away and says in distress, "We're missing dinner." You comfort them and tell about your plans to escape the Dreaming Dog through the grotto. They tell you, "Yes, I'll follow you. This place is dark. I fear we won't last long here. The Dog takes it out of you, one weary bite at a time." "OK," you say, "I just have to go back to my room and get my stuff. Come on." You take your partner's hand in yours and it makes you strong and together you fly down the path with the wind at your backs toward the looming shadow of the inn. When you reach it, you enter through the laundry, which is empty during the dinner hour. You know they are aware of your absence from the dining hall because you two hide beneath a table with a cloth on it as two of the burly guards with tiny heads, like nipples with eyes and mouths, screech and warble about how not only are you wanted by the inn but Gas has just arrived from the mountain claiming you left him to die and he's murderously angry.

The weird search party moves on, and you sneak down empty hallways to your room. By the time you reach it, it is almost 7:00 p.m. Another minute and people will be everywhere at the inn. You hurriedly put your pack together and your partner helps you. All is ready. You head for the door and suddenly stop. Your partner isn't moving. They tell you that in the time they've been waiting for you at the Dreaming Dog, they've gotten hooked on Pistol Witch. "I'm going to need to take a stash of it with us and work my way off it. But if I try to quit like that," they say and snap their fingers, "it'll kill me." "OK," you say, because you will promise them anything; meanwhile you hear voices outside returning to the rooms and gardens from dinner.

Together you smash in three doors to three different rooms and easily find the Witch stash in each room. The operation takes mere minutes and you're dragging your partner out of the last room as they're reaching back to pocket the pipe and matches, when who should appear at the door to block your escape? That's right, Gas. Gaspar Maloney, with the two nipple heads backing him up, toting electric cattle prods and pistols. You two retreat up against the wall, and Gas gets closer. "Oh, you're gonna touch it," he says and points his leather flesh at you. "After I make them touch it," he says over his shoulder, "shoot them both dead and bury them out in the Mushroom Garden. I'll trip on the red caps that grow from the loam of their disintegration." Gas takes a step toward you, and you ready yourself to resist his efforts.

And in that instant, the entire inn gives a shiver, distant cries fill the air, and a loudspeaker sounds from under the couch of the room you've broken into. An announcement is broadcast throughout the room, echoing throughout the inn. "The dog is dreaming. I repeat, the dog is dreaming. Run for your lives." The inn explodes with the sound of a stampede, everyone heading for the exits. Gas forgets his revenge and he and the guards take off. Your partner tells you to run and that the dream of the dog is an agonizing death. You run, side by side, the opposite direction from the crowd mobbing the hallway. Every foot forward is a battle against the tide. You're heading for the library and the spiral bone staircase into the grotto. Eventually the crowds thin and you can make your way. Your partner warns you that when the green dog of the inn dreams, he sends out a pack of dream dogs that devour the customers, taking some kind of ethereal sustenance from their captured souls. The inn is merely a trap, a place for the dream dogs to feed when hungry. As you turn the last corner for the library, you see one of the creatures, peeling, with its teeth, the outer film of reality from a screaming Shell Tock.

The wispy blur of the creature peels the poor fellow like an onion, completely devouring every layer with misty fangs sharper than bone. You watch Tock vanish before your eyes; every scream more terrible the less of him there is. "Watch," your partner whispers in your ear when there is but one more mouthful of prey. The dream dog eats it and lays down to sleep. As it touches the floor, its green miasma disappears. You run past where the horrifying spectacle took place, and it's as if nothing ever happened there. You enter the library, find the door to the spiral stairs, and the two of you descend. Behind you, at barely a distance, comes the sound of the pack bearing down. The dream dogs are on the stairs, gliding step to step like nimble dancers.

You are at the edge of the pool; the approaching howls and yips resound off the rock walls. You take each other's hands and leap, and the moment you touch the warm water, the blind fish flee, taking their light and warmth, and you plunge down and down. Frantically you grope for an escape beyond the boundary of the inn. But soon enough you realize the blind fish will not be leading you with their light, there is no escape from the Inn of the Dreaming Dog, there is no Source of Glory. Stop struggling, put your arms around each other tight, and fall into the dark together.

Monkey in the Woods

When I first heard about it, I was like, "Yeah, OK." Then my brother told me he'd actually seen it swing from branch to branch off into distant trees. I liked the idea of it even if it wasn't true. But I eventually saw it, a few days after Christmas, staring down at me from high in a maple only a few hundred yards behind the school. It had a white beard and bushy white eyebrows, a little embroidered vest, a red fez with a chin strap. Its canines were curved. The tail was long and ended in a Q, like the beginning of a knot. Its foot hands clung to a branch, and its free hand pointed a finger at me. It screamed, eyes bulging, and I fled.

I'd seen that monkey only five months earlier. It was part of a traveling summer carnival that set up in Brightwaters every year, two towns east. The scene was corn dogs, scumbags and sketchy rides, one of which was called The Round Up. It used centrifugal force by spinning people so fast they stuck to the wall of the contraption and then the bottom fell out. This kid in my class, Leacock, took a turn at it and puked. The vomit went right down the curving row of spinners and smacked each one in the face. I stayed away from those rides due to a story I'd heard on my transistor radio. It was about a girl who went on a summer carnival attraction called The Twister and got her long hair caught in the machinery. The Twister twisted it right off her head along with her scalp.

There was an organ-grinder making the rounds at the fairground of the carnival in Brightwaters, and he had a monkey on a thin, six-foot chain. It stole people's food, and if they complained, the thing would climb up their clothing and punch them between the eyes. My brother got punched by it and he said its fist was hard as a nail. The last night before the carnival pulled up stakes and moved on, I was there, and saw a dark-haired woman come stumbling out of the crowd and whirling lights in a red dress. She had her hand to her face and blood was seeping around her fingers. Somebody she knew called to her, "Joan, what happened?" and she said, "That fuckin' monkey bit my face."

That woman, Joan, had them call the cops on Giacomo (that was the monkey's name). I stayed as long as I could, but my father was sitting in the Biscayne out under the tall dark trees, reading the horse paper, and I promised him I'd be back in an hour and a half. The cops arrived as I was running to the car. On my way, I stopped for a moment and wormed into a crowd that had formed around Giacomo and his owner. The old man was cowering at the center of the ring. People were red in the face, screaming at him. The monkey intermittently laughed and bent over to pat its ass, long tail wriggling like a snake. The chant "Kill it!" chased me as I raced across the dirt parking lot.

At Christmastime, two nights prior to the big day, snow falling outside the living-room window, by the glow of the tree's blue light my brother whispered to me so the adults in the dining room drinking wouldn't hear, "Martin Gompers saw a monkey in the woods today."

"Where?"

"Pretty far in. Almost to the sugar sand, swinging from branch to branch like Tarzan."

"Gompers is an idiot," I said.

You'd think, right then, though, when my brother told me what Gompers said, I would immediately recall the incident at the carnival with Giacomo, but no, I never did. Months had passed and it was Christmas time and snowing and we were free from school and presents were in the offing. Besides, Gompers was a large lumpen nitwit with a bowl haircut and buck teeth. In gym class one day he strangled me until I managed to kick him in the shins and run. I never put it together that the woods the sighting took place in was large and ranged east across two towns and ended right at the field where the Brightwaters carnival was held each summer.

In the days after Christmas, when kids were in the snowy woods trying out new BB guns and hiding from their parents, there came further reports of a monkey. This time from a reputable source. Supposedly the beast threw a handful of acorns down onto Daisy Cooper, girl genius. She thought it meant the monkey was hungry. The next day she brought apples and peanut butter sandwiches to the same spot near the bend in the stream where the sassafras trees grew. She looked up and told the monkey to come down and eat. The monkey screamed at her until she left. After I heard that story, I pictured her at night, in her pajamas, in her bedroom, writing about it in her diary.

Two weeks went by, and at least every other day there was a new sighting either in the woods or around the houses on its perimeter. There was one Wednesday when there were four sightings. My brother kept me apprised of all the monkey gossip. He was two years older and had friends. On New Year's Eve, all the neighbors came to our house. My mother played the piano, and the drinks were flowing. I stole some whiskey sour from the blender and ate a handful of maraschino cherries. Mr. Makanan from next door was half in the bag, which was halfway to how far he usually was in the bag. He was talking to my father, and I walked over and sat down.

"Did you hear all the hubbub about a monkey in the woods behind the school?" he asked and then burped with his mouth closed. I nodded and my father shook his head. Makanan had blubbery lips and was a tad breathless. Still he pressed on and said, "I was at the carnival this past summer and there was an incident wherein a woman I happen to know, my secretary, was assaulted by the organ-grinder's monkey. I tell ya, that monkey bit the *wrong* woman. Joany's a bitch on wheels. Had the cops there, the whole thing. She was threatening lawsuits. The owner of the carnival made a deal with her. If he killed the monkey and he let her watch it die, would she relent on the legal action? She agreed."

Makanan pulled himself to his feet, ice cubes clinking in his glass, and said, "Be back with a refill." I was intrigued by the story, but it was late, past midnight, and I leaned back and into my father. The cigarette smoke and the faint aroma of machining oil that never left him were like a magic sleep perfume to me. We watched the snow outside, fat flakes falling through the light of the streetlamp across the way. I eventually dozed off and was somewhere between sleep and waking when I heard above the low music and conversation of the guests Makanan's voice. Even as deep in as I was, I could tell he was yet more loaded. I heard and envisioned whatever he spoke.

He stayed with Joan and her two sons until after the carnival had closed down and the rides were locked up. In the pitch dark, they were ushered by the carnival clown, fake nose and makeup still on him, into a clearing in the woods beyond the field. Someone handed him a flashlight that hardly cut the night. Giacomo's owner was there and three of the carnival workers who ran the rides; each had a shotgun. The carnival owner had a pistol in a holster on his belt. Giacomo's hands were tied with cord behind his back. He stood against the trunk of a giant oak lit by the headlamps of a tractor. Joan's kids were crying at the fact that their mom was going to have a monkey killed. She told them, "Shut it." They grew quiet, but the tears still rolled. "Gentlemen?" she said.

"Ready," said the head of the carnival.

The organ-grinder dropped to his knees as the three shotguns rose to aim dead center on Giacomo's heart. The monkey somehow knew it was in a bad spot and its teeth were chattering. The owner took out his pistol and aimed as well, but before he could give the order to fire, the organ-grinder said something, one word, a command in whatever language was his, and in an instant, Giacomo was free. Before the cord that had bound him hit the ground, he was streaking toward his firing squad.

One stupendous leap and he was on the face of the middle shooter. With his back foot he kicked the double barrel of the shotgun and it went off and sprayed the first shooter's knee, ripping his pants to bloody shreds. With a wild scream from both the monkey and his victim, the middle shooter's left eye came out of its socket on the sharp fingers of Giacomo. The head of the carnival stared in astonishment, his mouth wide and dark as a cavern's. The monkey used the one-eyed man's shoulders as a platform from which to leap up and grab a low-hanging branch. While the poor middle shooter fell to the ground to join the first shooter, the third shooter took aim. Before he could pull the trigger, a prodigious rain of monkey shit fell on Joan, her sons, the three shooters, the organ-grinder, the head of the carnival, and Mr. Makanan.

As the snow subsided, so did sightings of the monkey. He may have been hiding among the thick branches of a pine. That was my brother's theory. I didn't want to picture Giacomo dead, that snarling face finally slack with peace at the blue heart of a snow drift he'd fallen into from the branches high above. I don't think Gompers ever gave up on seeing Giacomo. I bet if I were to run into him today, he'd lean close to me, suck on those big fucking horse chompers, and whisper with a misty chaser of spit, "There's a monkey in the woods." A touching report came from Dean Fuscia, who lived next to the school. He said he was walking home one night in January, and in the light of the upstairs window in the house across the street from his, where the old woman who sometimes went door to door through the neighborhood and asked for a glass of gin, lived, he saw the monkey plain as day and it was done up in a blue dress with puffy shoulders and a high collar.

The other person who wasn't willing to let Giacomo become a memory was Mrs. Cooper. She, of course, stole into Daisy's room while her daughter was in school and read every word of the girl's diary. Daisy was a good writer, I remember from being in class with her, and I'm guessing she rendered her affection for Giacomo in terms she never would for her mother. In any event. Mrs. Cooper brought it to the PTA and demanded someone do something about it.

"What do you want me to do?" asked Mr Torrey, the principal.

"Hire a hunter."

Torrey laughed, but Mrs. Cooper stoked monkey fear throughout the neighborhood at every Tupperware party and after church, and eventually Torrey was forced to make a compromise. His plan was to get a few of the men whose kids went to the school together and go out in the woods with guns and hunt the monkey down. Daisy's mother agreed to his proposal. Somehow my father got roped into the hunting party. It was not his kind of thing by a long shot, but my mother forced him to it out of a sense of civic duty. "Shit," was what he said to her to confirm he'd participate. At the end of February, on a 55-degree Saturday, sunny, with a slight breeze, the hunt was on. Kids were not allowed in the woods. It had been announced at school over the loudspeaker before the pledge on Friday morning. Any kid caught in the woods on Saturday would have detention for the summer during summer-school hours. The thought of spending July and August locked up every morning in a hot room with nothing to do but stare at the concrete walls was enough to keep us away.

On Sunday morning, while he drank coffee and read the horse paper, I asked my father if they shot the monkey.

"Yeah, we bagged him," he said.

"Did he die fast?"

"Not fast enough for my money. It was pretty cold out there."

"Did he cry?"

"I don't know. What's his name, the guy with the mustache and glasses, brought his .22 rifle. The monkey was in midair. The guy, oh yeah, Mr. Donnely, hit him right in the chest. The monkey dropped into the pond. We fished him out and the cops took him away." He lit a cigarette and went back to his paper, working figures in the margins with a stub of a pencil. What my father told me was reported by Torrey to the PTA at the very next meeting, garnering a round of applause. I imagine Mrs. Cooper's triumph was undercut by the fact that her daughter now disliked her even more.

The draw of life's current was strong and eventually pulled me on, but not before I spent a day or so wondering how Giacomo had gone bad. I wondered what happened to the organ-grinder. He wasn't much of a draw without the crazy monkey. Who needed an old man who didn't speak English wandering around a fairground playing songs on a box with a crank handle? The tunes were stale, like something from a splintered, rickety carousel. What made the monkey so angry? I don't think the old man abused him. He wasn't afraid of Giacomo but instead treated him like a son he didn't know what to do with. Before my reverie was over, I pictured the monkey, in pajamas, in his room at night, writing in his diary about Daisy Cooper.

A few years passed and I was seventeen, a senior in high school. The carnival stopped appearing in Brightwaters the year I was fourteen, which would have been 1969. I remember because I was gonna ask Daisy to go with me. Instead we hitchhiked to the beach. That last year at home, I got a job working in a metal shop down by the tracks on the way to Babylon. It was at that job that I met Tom Mason. Forty, forty-five, maybe? The guy never wore a shirt unless it was freezing out. He'd work on the grinder and sparks would bounce off his flesh. Tom had a big ego and big muscles. He had twin dragon tattoos that grew up from his abdomen and intertwined while their twin maws flashed sharp blue teeth poised to bite his nipples. A scary dude, but fun enough to talk to at lunch or for a smoke break.

One day, when I got back from lunch early, he was sitting outside against the wall of the shop. I stopped and bummed a cig off him. He said to me, "Did I tell you about the time I helped execute a monkey?" The instant the words left his mouth I thought of Giacomo. I sat down next to him. "Where?" I asked. Holding his cig in two fingers, he pointed over his head due east. "Right over here in Brightwaters," he said. "Was it Giacomo?" I asked. He laughed. "Yeah, did you know that little fuck knuckle?"

I nodded. "I was there the night he bit that lady's face."

"Get the fuck out," he said. "Yeah I worked there running one of the rides."

"Which ride?"

"The Round Up."

"You mean where you go in circles and then the floor falls out?"

"That's it."

I told him the Leacock story and he said, "Oh yeah, I could make at least one person puke per session just how I adjusted the speed and then slammed on the brakes. After they'd stagger off, I'd just throw some sawdust on the puke and rev it up again for the next crowd."

"The way I heard it," I said. "Giacomo got away."

"Who told you that?"

"I forget."

"Nah, we shot the crap out of old Giacomo. To be honest, nobody felt too bad about it. He was a monumental pain in the ass. Steal your cigarettes, your wallet, your booze, and if you weren't careful, your girl." I pictured Daisy in her bikini with her thumb out on the side of the road, Giacomo pulling over in a Corvette Stingray to pick her up. Tom went on, "He's buried in a little clearing of trees just beyond the field where the carnival was held. He was shot up pretty bad, and we buried him on the spot where he fell. The organ-grinder knelt down next to the body and straightened Giacomo's puffy pants and little bowler derby with the chin strap. He placed a big rock on top of the grave, telling us, "So he does not rise from the dead."

"Wait," I said. "Giacomo didn't wear like a little jacket and fez?"

"I never saw him in that," said Tom. It struck me that if what Mason was telling me was true, then all my memories of Giacomo were false, including my sighting of him in the maple tree. If not the monkey, what did I see?

When I got home from work that night, I found my father out back, grilling his meal of a hundred meats—burgers, hot dogs, sausage, chicken . . . He was just getting the meat on, so nobody was outside with him at the picnic table yet. I told him I knew that story he told me about the death of Giacomo the monkey was a lie. He flicked his cigarette into the grill, dropping the ashes with a masterful touch between a sausage and a chicken leg.

At first, he didn't remember the incident, but eventually his mind came around to it. "We never went in the woods that day. We sat in Torrey's office and drank scotch, a bunch of us. It was a lot of fun. Then he made us swear to tell our kids that the hunting party had taken care of the monkey."

"He never believed in Giacomo?" I asked.

"He never gave a shit whether there was a monkey or not. In his office that day, a bunch of the guys from the neighborhood getting bombed on his booze, he told us that he was in the Break Out at St. Lo. He was a messenger and had to run for miles on dead bodies to get a message back to Patton whose Third Army was reinforcing. After that, a monkey in the woods is the least of your problems."

On Sunday, the only day both of us were off from work, my father drove us over to the field in Brightwaters. We took a couple of shovels with us and we went back into the woods and found the clearing Tom Mason had told me about. Right in the middle of it there was the rock the organ-grinder had placed on Giacomo's grave. I dug and he smoked and then he dug and I smoked, and eventually we found the monkey's remains. There was still a lot of hair and the bones were full of shot. The skull was shattered and yet still clung together. We found his bowler derby, the elastic band intact.

"Think of all the stories people told themselves and others about this monkey," I said. *Even Daisy,* I thought. *Even me.*

My father looked down at what was left of Giacomo and then up into the trees. "You know, there's always a monkey in the woods," he said.

The Match

I got a letter in the mail and read it while I ate dinner at the kitchen counter. Lynn, working on her mosaic, sat at the table by the sliding screen door, cracking green plates with a monkey wrench. Between the bashings of dishware, bird sounds came in from outside and a cool breeze sifted through.

"Listen to this," I said to her.

She lifted her goggles and turned to face me.

"From the way I'm reading it, the university says that if I want to continue teaching part time, I have to pass a test."

"Like the SAT?"

"No, it says I have to wrestle an angel. And they give me a date and time as to when this is all going to go down in the basement of the university library. It informs me here that the hallway will be darkened."

She barely heard the end of it from laughing. "Who sent you that?"

I shook my head.

"It has to be somebody from work, one of the other teachers."

"It's on official letterhead from the president's office."

"That doesn't mean shit," she said. "And besides, wrestle an angel? The only thing you're wrestling is your pants when you try to get into them."

"I was on wrestling in high school, but I sucked pretty bad. I do lift weights every other day, though."

"You're 65, you just got over hip surgery not too long ago, you've got diabetes, and you're overweight."

"I'll grab him by the throat and choke him out. Feathers'll fly."

"What are you getting so excited about? It has to be a joke."

"It's like the story from the Bible. Jacob wrestled the angel."

"Why?"

"I forget. I just know he was old, had two wives, two servants, and they were on the lam for some reason."

"Two wives?" said Lynn.

"A metaphor for teaching Composition."

Through the week, I contacted, by email, the few professors I was friendly with and asked if they'd sent the letter. Everyone of them told me the same thing, "No, it was the administration. You really do have to wrestle an angel."

"How come no one tells you about this when you get hired?" I wrote back.

All of them used this exact phrase when responding—*The surprise is half the battle.* I asked them to tell me about what it was like, but, of course, they all swore they were sworn to secrecy. Their advice: "Hire a trainer."

"In case you forgot, in my previous position, I was a full professor with an extensive list of publications," I wrote back to them, but by a lack of response, it was obvious they didn't give a shit.

Lynn was against the idea of me getting a trainer. "Tell them to fuck off and just start getting your social security. It's two part-time classes, not like you're pulling down six figures. Kick back and write a novel, join a club, volunteer at the hospital."

"It's only a grand for a trainer," I said.

She scowled as only she can.

"You should see these guys who have obviously beaten the angel," I told her. "They still have their jobs. Flimsy dudes. All nerdy. Not only them, but there's a woman, Kay Cass, who's confined to a wheelchair, and she's an adjunct who's been there longer than me, so she must have beaten the angel too. It can't be that fuckin' hard."

"So, why do you need a trainer? Ditch that idea."

"What, and train myself?"

"You can do it," she said.

"Well, I do have two weeks. That should be enough."

That night was a Friday, so we sat out on the porch and got hammered on wine. Me, red. Lynn, white. We played the little cylinder of a music box on Pandora's Nat King Cole station. It was spring and things were starting to blossom. The stars were out. The dogs and cats lay around us, sleeping. We reminisced about our long-ago days at the Colonial Motor Inn on Vestal Parkway in upstate New York. "Those were the days," she said, and I had a flashback of cooking hot dogs in a toaster oven in the bathroom, pissing on noodles in the toilet, and shaving on ketchup-puddled plates.

"Remember when Tom caught that guy peeping in the windows, ran him down in the graveyard, tied him to a chair, and threatened to shoot arrows into him?" she asked.

"Oh yeah, memories to warm an old age," I whispered. It got quiet then while we listened to "The Very Thought of You," Nat belting it out into the lonesome Ohio darkness, across the sprouting fields. When he was done, she asked me, "So, when's training start?"

"I have to take this seriously," I said. "With that money, I can put off retiring until I'm 67 or 68 and get more from Social Security for those later, golden years."

"Pushups?" she asked.

"I figure that's out of the question."

"Jogging some every day? Maybe, walking? . . . Crawling?"

"A brisk walk to the mailbox in the evening," I offered.

"What's your overall plan?"

"I've been thinking about it and decided the preparation should be more philosophical, you know, spiritual."

"Meditation?"

"Maybe."

The next day, despite a crushing hangover, I dove into the internet and looked up angels. I saw a depiction of an angel from the 15th century carrying what looked like a frisbee, pics of Bruno Ganz from *Wings of Desire,* the archangel, Michael, done up in armor with a sword—typical Christian vision of a badass. There were baby angels dragging Christ to heaven, white wings amidst the clouds, *Charlie's Angels,* and a piece by Maimonidies on *Wikipedia* about how "disembodied minds exist which emanate from God and are the intermediaries between God and all the bodies [objects] here in this world."

I turned the computer off and took a nap. It was summer vacation, no more marking papers for a while, no more Composition. The whole angel thing seemed ridiculous after my research. I just wanted the days to pass in mundane majesty, reading obscure books, writing stories, watching Lynn work in the garden during daylight, and drinking with her on the porch at night. After that, I rarely gave the angels another waking thought.

I did, however, dream of one. Every couple of nights, I'd be teaching at the University of the Land of Nod, the class made up of all the hard-case students I'd ever had in Comp. classes stretching back forty years. Sitting in the front row was this angry kid who had been diagnosed with a terminal disease—his heart grew more brittle by the day and would eventually just shatter. He knew he was going to die in the next five years. Stevie was his name. Bitter as could be and who could blame him?

Sitting behind him was Cindy, the girl who, when she got her period, suffered amnesia. She never knew what the fuck was going on. What can you do? When all was said and done, I gave her a B. The suicide and the murderer were in the row behind her. The former only wrote out contracts for First Alert, the latter, about a dragon named Flamer. The guy without legs, who rode around on a skateboard and walked on his hands, was in the back up on top of one of the desks. There were another ten, one more disconcerting than the next. But, hey, I'm a veteran, so even in dreamland I just buckled down to it. First up was a lecture on the difference between abstract and concrete detail.

Two nights later, I was back to teaching in my sleep in the basement of the library. In the middle of talking about gerund phrases, the classroom door opened and in walked a guy in a brown cassock; white wings jutting out the back. His hair was scraggly and his halo was a sick green, blinking on and off as if God's grace was shorting out. He came to one of the empty seats, sat and faced me.

"You're late," I said. "Class has already begun."

That's when I noticed his face was totally fucked up. Rumpled and twisted, his lips resembled a parrot beak, and his eyes were looking in completely opposite directions. The sight of him was so startling, I withdrew two steps to the blackboard.

"Saint Drogo at your service," he said. "Here to train you."

The students were all trying not to look at the horrid saint. My first thought was that he might actually be the devil. "I never asked for a trainer," I said.

"Send the students home. We have work to do."

"I think I'm supposed to be teaching them."

"Come on, let's get a move on," he said. He did this trick where he was both at the back of the classroom and at the exit in the front at the same time. As the students walked, staggered, hobbled, and crawled into the darkness outside the door, he'd smack each of them in the back of the head and they'd ascend swiftly as if picked up by the funnel of a black tornado. The last out was the kid who I recalled had written about the death of his brother—"Flattened like a pancake by a truck on a street in Brooklyn." Part of that paper was about his having lived chained to a radiator for the rest of his childhood. Drogo gave him a boot in the ass. The darkness swept him away. The door slammed closed behind him.

The saint approached me and I sat in my chair behind the desk to feel less exposed. He thrust his face in mine and said,

"Let's get one thing clear. I know I'm ugly as sin, but I can help you prepare. Do you have any idea who you'll be wrestling?"

I shook my head, averting my gaze from him. His halo buzzed and sparked.

"Metatron."

"Metatron? Isn't that a Transformer?"

He backed off a little, "No, you're thinking of Megatron. This is Metatron, the cause of causes, the primordial, the tenth and last emanation, the prince of the present, angel of the veil, ancient of days. If angels had a god, he would be it. But they don't 'cause there's only one god."

"I'm having a hard time following you," I told him.

"I know. At the bottom it all just gets murky and then what the fuck?" He flapped his wings twice and said, "Let's get started. Metatron was only ever known to speak one thing: 'I have been young, also, I have been old.'"

"What's that mean?"

"Don't worry. Nobody knows. What you need to remember, though, is that his skin is fire, his eyelashes are lightning, his breath has the corrosive properties of Time. At the center of his mind is the first moment of the universe, a light so powerful it will make the blind see, and then blind them, only to cure them and blind them again."

Drogo snapped his fingers and I was sitting at a rooftop bar. The angel was making drinks with a sweating chrome shaker. "I call this one Purple Deuces. Two parts fruit of paradise. One-part earthly desire. A jigger of the Holy Ghost's regret, a dash of the tears of Eve. And there you go."

"What's the name have to do with it?"

"That fruit of paradise makes you shit purple." And to my horror, I did, all the next day. I wanted to tell Lynn how my dreams were affecting reality but it sounded pretty insane. So I kept it to myself. Two nights later I was back at the rooftop bar. Drogo was mixing the Deuces. "OK, let's get started," he said and poured the chilled purple syrup into a martini glass—garnished with a piece of dried quince at the end of a toothpick. "Tell me more about the kid with the heart of glass."

"Is this part of the training?"

"I'm just curious about these dead souls you're unpacking in your dreams."

"Stevie? He was a trip. Big thick glasses. A face like Alfred E. Neuman. I'd try to teach him basic sentence structure. I'd say, "Come on, you can get this." In his shrill voice, he'd say something like, "Of course I can. But if you were gonna die in five years would you give a shit about any of this stuff?" Sometimes he'd pitch a fit, but he was confined to a wheelchair and very frail. Occasionally, he'd knock somebody else's books on the floor. I'd tell him, "If you keep that up, I'm gonna have to get rid of you." He'd stop. Later, while the other students worked on their essays, I'd go sit with him ten or fifteen minutes before the class ended, and we'd talk about anything except writing or dying."

"In the long run, though," said Drogo, "you really didn't help him?"

I shook my head. "He's long gone. But I think about him all the time, and when I do, I picture his heart exploding like a bright red Christmas ornament, shattering to glittery bits."

"That was pretty much his fate," said the angel. "He never learned to write."

"I suppose I failed miserably then."

"Neither here nor there," said Drogo.

"What's my wrestling an angel have to do with my teaching? I don't get it."

"That's why you wrestle. To find out," he said and disappeared.

The rooftop bar dissolved beneath me. I fell twenty stories and woke, suddenly, in my bed. After that night, I dreamt of covered bridges, the lost and forgotten books of my favorite writers, that weird other house with the green shutters, and food gone bad. St. Drogo was bilocating in two other places than my dreams.

It was Wednesday night, so Lynn and I sat out on the porch and got hammered. There was a light drizzle and a strong breeze. We'd had music on but the speaker had run out of juice. Instead the symphony of wind chimes filled in. Two of the dogs slept, but Nellie, the psycho collie/shepherd mix, was standing at the edge of the top step of the porch, peering out into the dark, quietly growling. We'd recently seen a fox, and there was the raccoon family in the white oak across the field, the possum behind the shed, deer heading for the pear trees in the way back.

"Coyotes?" said Lynn.

"Or angels," I said.

"Yeah, I forgot about that. When is it?"

"This week some time. I have to go check the letter."

"Are you nervous?"

"I don't know what to expect, so it's hard to get nervous about it. I know I'm wrestling Metatron."

"Sounds like a machine," she said.

"His skin is fire and his breath is as corrosive as Time."

She rocked back in her chair and laughed.

"Think about wrestling something like that. Supposedly his eyelashes are lightning."

"Just quit," she said.

"I want to see what the deal is. If that angel of fire shows up, I'll quit on the spot. Obviously, I'm not wrestling that fuckin' thing. But I have a theory. Maybe the whole affair is just some ritualistic event, like a symbolic recognition of a milestone in your career. And the threat of the coming match makes you reconsider your life in teaching. When it's over, you either stay on and teach longer, or you throw in the towel. There's only one thing I don't get."

"What's that?"

"I'm not even religious. I don't go to church. I don't give two about the angels. And I was never aware, after having taught at the university for nearly ten years, that the place was in any way overtly religious."

"Wasn't the guy it's named after some famous Protestant?"

"If I lose the job, will you think less of me?"

"I'm the one who's telling you to forget about it. Just retire."

"We'll see," I said. That night I fell asleep in my chair on the porch and only woke at dawn to birdsong. I looked over and, in the dim light, I could see Lynn had gone in to bed. Then I heard footsteps and felt the planks beneath my feet tremble. A black bag went over my head, and I felt a needle in the neck. As I passed out, my body was being lifted by many hands amid the beating of wings.

I felt something hit against my back. Each jab was accompanied by a mechanical sound. For a moment I thought they were attaching wings, but then I came fully around and could ascertain that I was on the floor in the darkened hallway in the basement of the university library.

"Mr. Ford? Are you OK?" came a voice from behind me.

I turned to see it was Kay Cass. She'd been nudging me with her wheelchair. I stood up and staggered to catch my balance. Whatever had been in the hypo left a sweet taste like rose-petal candy. "I'm fine. I've just been burning the candle at both ends lately trying to get my pedagogy put together for the fall." She gave me a look like she knew I had no idea what pedagogy meant. I flashed her a smile and said, "You know why I'm down here, right?"

"What are you talking about?" she asked.

"I think my match is this morning."

"What match?"

I leaned over and whispered, "Wrestling the angel."

"Don't get so close," she said, putting her hands up to block my hot wine breath. "What are you talking about?"

"You never wrestled the angel?"

"What angel?" The wheelchair whirred and she backed out of the hallway, wearing an expression that led me to believe I'd freaked her out. Quiet filled the darkness. I could hear my blood pumping. I turned and saw, at the opposite end of the hall, a small flame spark to life in the pitch black. The red orange tongue sang in a chorus as it grew into the form of a man with wings. I was numb at the sight of it. The only thing going through my mind were the words "I quit." My voice wouldn't work to say them, though. The music swelled and Metatron spoke a rasher of incomprehensible/Ancient of Days bullshit, working himself into a lather that would peak with, I supposed, him lunging at me.

His face was a face of faces amid the fire. The flames shifted from one personality and visage to another. I watched the anger grow in him. I looked him over. He wasn't any taller than me. He was in better shape, though, and seemed eager to tussle. I thought if I could just get a grip on his throat, I could push him back and take the advantage. I'd follow that with some uppercuts to the ribs. Maybe a karate chop to the side of the head. I was high on my prospective agility and defensive strategies until he stamped his foot and the building shook. I'm not sure I didn't crap my pants. Metatron's breathing reverberated and then, in my voice, he said, "If I lose, will you think less of me?" His words were followed by cackling laughter.

It was then that I thought "Fuck Metatron" and bum-rushed him. Before I got halfway down the hall, I was gasping for breath. Still, I managed to reach him and grab him by the throat before he could react. Yes, the fire burned, and it hurt bad, but its drawbacks could never exceed the joy of throttling Metatron against the file cabinets at the end of a dark hall. One, two, I slammed him with body shots to the ribs, twenty years' worth of teaching behind each one. His breath was electric with the stink of paradise. It was in administering the karate chop to the side of his head that I remembered that I didn't know karate and all along had been envisioning a scene from the opening credits of *Mannix*, a '70s detective TV show. He moved like a flash, kicked me in the nuts, punched me in the jaw, clonked me on the head with a rock-like fist.

I staggered in the dark, dizzy and short of breath. In that brief period, I realized that although my hands were burned by the fire of his form, once I let go of him they were instantly healed, no scars. My inclination was for the floor, but the revelation about the fire rallied me and I turned it around. As he came in for the kill, I jabbed him twice in that shifting angel face, then brought the left around and clocked his fiery jaw. He staggered backward and when he began to fall his left leg was at an angle to the floor; I stomped on the shin, and whatever angels are made of, I heard it snap in two. He hit the deck, his fire went out, and he started moaning to beat the band. His skin was the consistency of burnt grocery-store pizza. Wafts and curls of smoke rose from him.

After a joyous moment, I felt bad for old Metatron, but figured I'd at least established the fact that I could literally beat him. The situation also offered me a chance to display my easier-going side. Who wouldn't dig a teacher with a heart of gold? I helped the big wreck onto his good leg. The other leg, from mid-shin down, hung like a dead fish in a sock, swinging here and there, every time he hopped alongside of me. His arm was draped across my shoulders. "You didn't have to break my leg," he said. He was crying from the pain.

"OK, whatever."

I found my way through the dark to my classroom door. Moving slowly and carefully I managed to set Metatron down in one of the student's seats. Then I made my way back to my desk. When I sat in my chair, I finally was able to catch my breath. Seeing was out of the question, though.

"Is there an angel ambulance I can call?" I asked him.

He said nothing. In fact, it had gotten so silent, I could no longer hear him panting from the pain. It suddenly dawned upon me that I could turn the lights on. I got out of my chair and crossed the room to the entrance. The switch was right there, inside the door. I found it and flipped it. The light was momentarily blinding, like the supposed beacon in Metatron's head. I cleared my eyes because sitting in the student seat, at the first table in front of my desk, wasn't the crisped form of the angel. It was, instead, a young woman. She appeared to either be sleeping or unconscious. For as little as I could see of her face, there was something familiar about her. I kept my eyes on her as I went to my desk and sat again.

I moved back through my mind, swiping the cobwebs aside, descending into the past. Somewhere in my search, I realized she had been a student at one time, back in my old community college teaching days. The department head put her in my class halfway through the semester. I'd long forgotten her name. She was maybe nineteen, dark bangs, always dressed in overalls and a sweater, always sporting a necklace of candy, like a choker, to cover the scars on her throat. She stared at the wall a lot, and wrote maybe a handful of sentences the couple of months she came to class. She was definitely out of it. Next time I saw my department chair, I asked him if he was going to start wheeling the students in on gurneys. He told me, "It's open enrollment. As long as they have high school diplomas, they're in."

I ignored her limitations and made a good effort to reach her and get her to do a little writing. It was a slow, sad business, with tiny victories of a line or two, followed by disheartening retreats into silent staring. Sometimes the tears would roll fat and glistening down her face as she no doubt struggled to find herself within. I'd try to talk to her, and during one of those sessions, she managed to get out that she had a dog. It was a subject she seemed to respond to, and although those sessions weren't much more animated than the usual, they usually resulted in a few broken and twisted lines of writing.

One day her brother dropped her off for class. I introduced myself to him and asked if he could hang out for just a few minutes. He agreed. I got the students started on a project and then I spoke to him out in the hallway. He told me that she'd been in a car accident and the oxygen to her brain was cut off for a while. After telling me that, he said, "A long while." I caught his drift. I asked why she came to school, since it sounded like her condition was pretty bad. He told me, "My parents had her in their old age. They don't want to deal with her being around all day, so they enrolled her here. Plus, sometimes when she doesn't get out for a while, she gets violent." By the time he left, I wished I hadn't asked. Also, it came out that she didn't have a dog.

In the weeks before she phantomed, she was never any trouble. In fact, a slow as molasses, meandering conversation with her about her dog that didn't exist could really keep me centered and her smiling that vacant smile. We had quite a few. She never returned from winter break. On the last class before the holiday, after the room had emptied and I was gathering together my books and chalk, I discovered something when I lifted the paperback dictionary I always put out on my desk at the start of every class. Beneath it was a tiny yellow disk with a hole in the center. I picked the thing up and turned it in my hand. It took a minute, but finally I realized it was one of the candies from her candy choker. I would normally just have assumed that the necklace had broken, but the fact that the disk was under the dictionary was a giveaway. She'd been the last one to use it that day, and I'd been surprised, as it was her first time borrowing the book.

I wished I might have remembered her name, and in trying to bring it back I was overwhelmed by the thought of thousands of students I'd taught through the years; how many were completely lost to me. Instead of waking her, I quietly turned off the lights and left the room. Groping my way down the hall, I made it to the main floor of the library. The place was shadowy and silent. Only the morning light streaming in the windows lit the place. It didn't seem to be open yet. Kay Cass was nowhere in sight, nor was anyone else. Don't ask me how, but my keys were in my pants pocket and my car was in the empty parking lot. I got in and drove home.

That evening, over wine, I told Lynn about the battle with Metatron, and about the girl who took his place.

"Did you hear from the school? Are you in or out?"

"They said I can keep teaching."

"Do you even want to?"

"Just a semester or two more," I said and rocked.

Lynn shrugged at my reply and we went back to our drinks, dozing into the night, while Crazy Nellie, the dog, stood watch against coyotes, possums, and angels.

From the Balcony of the Idawolf Arms

Willa hated Saturday nights. She had to leave the kids home alone with no babysitter. She knew they weren't old enough to be on their own, but there was no one nearby to help her. Their father was three states away and she wasn't unhappy about that. Every cent she made waitressing was apportioned before she even served the drinks and meals at Walsh's Diner. Only when the tips were great did she have enough to stow a few dollars away for an emergency. She'd never been a churchgoer growing up but now she prayed every night, primarily for the kids to stay healthy and to get to a better place and time. It had nothing to do with religion. Leaving them on their own was taking a big chance, but there wasn't any aspect of their life now that wasn't.

Landing the unexpected diner job was a godsend and with it she just managed, before the start of winter, to get out of the mothers and children shelter they'd landed in and into a crazy old apartment. It was at least warm and had a door that locked. The electricity and the water were erratic, the TV was dead, there was no shower in the bathroom, just an old tub with lion-claw feet, and the furniture smelled like a dog on a rainy day. Still, in its way, the old place was magnificent. The ceilings were ten feet or more, affording plenty of room to dream of a better future. And it was cheap—a red-brick leviathan from the early 1900s. Four stories with a tile roof. Some of the brick was chipping, a few of the windows on the bottom floor were cracked, the banisters were splintery, but otherwise the place looked pretty good for an old wreck. There were three-story wooden buildings on either side, both ramshackle and abandoned.

A copper plaque above the tall front door, its letters gone green, announced *The Idawolf Arms*. The real-estate person told her that the owner, who lived on the top floor, a Mr. Susi, had just opened the place up for rentals and was only renting the middle two floors. The first floor was a dingy lobby from way back when the place had been a small upscale hotel—dim lighting and sheets thrown over the furniture and front desk. It was spooky to walk through at night on the way up to the third floor. As of yet, there were no other boarders, but the owner had hopes to rent the remaining available rooms. Willa never met Mr. Susi, and the real-estate woman told her he was "somewhat reclusive."

Whereas Willa hated Saturday night, the kids, Olen and Dottie, looked forward to it. With Willa not there to scold or hug, there were any number of opportunities to be bad. They weren't, though. Even Dottie, the younger at eight, knew what was at stake. They perfectly grasped the dilemma their mother was in with work and not always being able to be there; how everything in their lives balanced on a knife blade. Willa cared so much and they could feel it. They wanted for it to be always like that. So, instead of running roughshod, breaking things and eating badly, they behaved and channeled their energy into a ritual built around a miracle of chance.

At the door, before leaving, Willa knelt down in front of the kids and once again went through the list of things they were absolutely not allowed to do—leave the apartment, open the door to strangers, cook anything on the stove. They could use the microwave to heat up their dinner, spaghetti in the refrigerator from two nights earlier.

"What if it's the cops at the door?" asked Dottie.

Willa remained patient and said, "Get a chair, stand on it, and look through the peep hole. If it's someone saying they are the cops and they're not dressed like cops, go and get in the bathroom and lock the door behind you."

"We'll be OK," said Dottie, sensing that even the thought of someone breaking in made her mother a nervous wreck.

Willa reached into the pocket of her blue-striped uniform and brought out a small bag of M&M's in each hand. "You can only eat these after dinner and if you're good," she said, and they all laughed at the absurdity of it. Then she slipped her coat on, kissed and hugged them, and went out the door. She waited to hear it lock behind her and then the kids listened to her footsteps on the creaky stairway heading down to the dark lobby. They bolted into the living room at the front of the apartment to look out the tall window. In the twilight they saw her heading up Rose Street, away from the dilapidated end of the city.

Olen went through the apartment and turned on all of the lights. Then he settled on the couch with the paperback he'd recently gotten at the local library used-book sale—*Watership Down.* Next to him, sitting on the floor, Dottie drew a portrait of a robot with a head like a lightning bolt with eyes and a square mouth.

"What's that one's name?" her brother asked her. He loved the crazy things she called her robots. There were dozens of the pictures laying around the apartment. After the drawing and the naming, there seemed nothing in it for her.

"This one is going to be Mrs. Shakes," she said, concentrating on keeping the pink crayon in the circle of the right eye. "She shakes and then electricity shoots out her ears."

"I don't see any ears on her," he said.

While looking him in the eye, she drew a C and a backwards C on either side of the robot's head. She laughed and gave him the finger.

An hour later, night had fallen and the children knew they had to get moving so as not to be late for the show. Olen put the spaghetti in the microwave and Dottie poured the milk. "Cheese?" she asked, putting the milk back in the fridge.

"You mean that white stuff in the shaker?" asked Olen. "That's not really cheese. That's the shaved-off callouses of an old man's feet."

"I used to eat it," said Dottie.

"What happened?"

"You."

Dinner was served. The spaghetti was partially cold, but they were so hungry they didn't even bother to put it back in the microwave. While they ate, they discussed the new school they were in. They'd been in a number of them in the two years since their father had left. "What's your teacher's name?" he asked her.

"Mrs. Beaglestretch."

"No way."

"That's her name," said Dottie. "Every day after lunch she goes in the coat closet at the back of the room and farts. We all hear her in there and everybody tries not to laugh."

"You're making that up."

She shook her head. "Who's yours?"

"Mr. Mace. The kids call him Mace Cut and Paste cause all he does is hand out sheets he makes on the copier that we have to fill out. He never teaches us anything; he just hands out sheets. He sits at his desk while we fill out the sheets and looks at his iPhone."

When they were finished with dinner, they scraped the plates into the kitchen garbage and set them in the sink. Sometimes they washed them and cleaned up the kitchen, but as it was, they were running a little late. By seven thirty, they were back at the front window looking down and scanning the sidewalks, watching for any movement beneath the only two streetlights in the neighborhood that still worked. "Like usual, you watch on the right and I'll watch on the left," he said.

"I always get the right," she said, disappointed.

"I always get the left. What difference does it make?"

"None, I guess," she said. A moment later she pointed quickly and said, "What's that?" But in an instant, they saw it was a kid on his bike, going in the opposite direction. Then there was a long spell of silent anticipation.

Around quarter to eight, Dottie spotted the black dog only a second before her brother did. Their mother had it from the real-estate lady that the animal's name was Nox. "He'll be coming soon," Olen whispered as if the person they expected in the street could hear her. Through the glass, above the wind and the rustling of the leaves in the giant sycamore that shaded the Idawolf Arms, they could hear the high-pitched whistle that flew up from the shadowy street and caused the dog to freeze in mid-step. Its master emerged out of the dark and into the glow of the streetlight in a black overcoat and black wide-brimmed hat. The ends of a long scarf were lifted behind him in the wind. Olen thought of him as a part of the night that stepped out of itself in the form of a man. Dottie thought of him only as Mr. Susi. They knew he was their upstairs neighbor. That simple name, though, had over the course of the last four Saturday nights come to inspire fear and wonder.

"Get the flashlight. I'll turn the lights out," he said. They scurried through the apartment and met at their mother's bedroom door in the dark, a thin penlight illuminating Dottie's face. Olen moved around the bed to the big window that looked out at the abandoned wooden building next door. Dottie followed. The sill for that window was a seat, with a ledge that came out three feet and a cushion on top. Olen noticed that Dottie had her blanket wrapped around her. He thought it a great idea and wished he'd gotten his, but the show was soon to start and he didn't want to miss a moment of it. She sat always on the right and he on the left, each with their back pressed against the wide frame.

"OK," he said when they were both in place. She turned off the flashlight and there came the sound of M&M's bags being torn open. All else was silent, and from where they sat, they could hear Mr. Susi use his key on the door in the lobby. They heard him on the steps, up all three flights, and heard the door to his place open and close. A moment later, they breathed deeply and a large circle of light appeared on the side of the old building not but ten yards away. A crisp bright circumference six feet wide and high. Following the light came music filtering down through the heating-duct system, "Mr. Susi's symphony music" their mother called it when she heard it whispering in the kitchen.

Olen and Dottie understood how it worked. After the first night they'd witnessed it, they were on the street the next day and happened to be in a position to see the upper story of the Idawolf Arms. On the top floor, in one of its rooms, there was a circular window, floor to ceiling. Olen explained to Dottie the effect. It all had to do with the way the room was lit. The bulb, no doubt set near the ceiling, projected whatever stood or moved in front of it as a silhouette which appeared one story down on the worn gray wood of the building across the alley. The silhouettes came through so clearly in the circle, the detail amazingly precise. After the first few glimpses of Mr. Susi's shadow passing by, the music somehow always took over and coordinated its slow, smooth rhythms to whatever was happening in the bright circle. It was only then that he appeared in full silhouette, standing at the center of the light in a shirt with long, puffy sleeves and a high collar. His hair was a tall wave about to break. They heard, very faintly from behind the music, the whistle that called the dog to him.

A thin, pointed stick appeared in his hand and he held it up like a maestro's baton and turned slowly in circles. Dottie realized for the first time, from his profile, that Mr. Susi had a beard. Nox followed him around, carefully watching the stick as if his master was about to throw it. Somewhere the music jumped to a faster pace just as the dog jumped to his hind legs. He bounced around and Susi held the baton up high just out of the reach of the creature's jaws. When he brought the baton down to his side, the music rolled slower, and as it devolved into a lullaby, it was as if the dog had gotten used to walking on its hind legs. He strode slowly back and forth in front of his master, stepping like a dainty clothes model. Both Olen and Dottie stopped chewing

M&M's as the face of Nox seemed to stretch and deform and then snap back into the silhouette of someone with long hair piled atop their head. In fact, the dog had transformed into the figure of a woman in a long dress. She opened her mouth wide and leaning toward Mr. Susi's left ear vomited a torrent of tiny butterflies that came like a raging creek and after swamping him from view swarmed upward and around the room like a murmuration of sparrows.

The music swept along in an elegant discordant waltz. Olen and Dottie had seen all this before, seen the tendrils grow from the woman's skin, seen the flowers blossom and their vines reach out for Mr. Susi who, producing a scissor from his pocket cut each feeler as it drew near. With every cut, agony registered in the woman's body with a jerk, a heaving of the chest, and the head thrown back to utter a whimper of toads that appeared on her lips and then leaped to the floor. Mr. Susi raised the scissor like a knife and stuck it in the side of the woman's head. Smoke puffed out and as it did she shrank back into a dog with human legs and arms. The kids had no words to describe what the meaning of it was, though they'd seen the same before on other Saturday nights. An icy ball of confusion spun behind their eyes. All through the weeks the strange imagery of these movies twisted through their days and surfaced in their dreams. What came next, though, was something new.

Nox lunged, his teeth bared and snapping. Susi's arms went up in the air and the dog\man took hold of his master's throat. There was a lightning jerk of the snout and dripping blackness as if a bottle of ink had spilled everywhere. In profile you could not only tell Mr. Susi had a beard but also that his throat had been ripped out. It was Olen who screamed. At the sound of it, Nox's head snapped to attention, and he dropped the lifeless body of his master to the floor. He undoubtedly drew toward the circular window, his shadow form gigantic in the bright circumference. "It's looking down here," whispered Dottie. "It heard you." With those words, the light upstairs went out, the music went off, and the alley fell back into darkness.

Neither Olen nor Dottie had anything to say. Their hearts were beating so loud they wondered if Nox could hear. They moved to the bed and huddled there, numb with fear, listening for the sound of the floorboards upstairs. Instead of footsteps, they heard the tap tap tap of dog claws. A stillness settled in and lasted so long their immediate fears melted slightly before there came a soft knocking at the apartment door. They held each other's hands and squeezed tight. Eventually, Olen moved, dragging Dottie along. He inched cautiously to the edge of the bed. They stepped down onto the floor as softly as possible. Neither wore shoes, only socks. They left their mother's room and made for the safety of the bathroom. In their journey through the dark, they had to pass the apartment door. They heard the thing breathing heavily. In a quiet but resonating voice it called, "Children, open up."

Dottie ran ahead to the bathroom and held the door, ready to slam it shut if she had to. Olen stopped in his tracks and turned to the dog/man's voice. "What are you?" he asked.

There was a low growling sound and the answer came back, "Different . . . and hungry."

A spark of fear shot through Olen and he sprinted to the bathroom. Dottie closed the door fast and locked it. Luckily the lights were working. They got in the tub and listened. Hours passed before they heard the tap tap tap of the dog claws on the way back up to the fourth floor. Mr. Susi's door opened and closed, and there descended a perfect stillness. It was only then that they dozed off to sleep.

They woke to the sound of their mother's voice at the door. Olen got up and unlocked it. Dottie was close behind him. They hugged her as hard as they could. Willa begged them to tell her everything. She led the way into the kitchen, and they took turns as she made coffee. They told about the movies; they told about

Nox and Mr. Susi. They didn't tell about that one night when Susi in silhouette appeared to be having sex with an octopus. Nobody mentioned that, nor the one scene where a cat was devoured by master and dog. Otherwise they told her everything. She sat at the table with her cup and lit a cigarette. Olen and Dottie sat across from her.

"Are you sure this is real?" said Willa. "It sounds like a monster movie." She took a long drag, coughed, and a tiny yellow butterfly fell out of her mouth into her coffee.

Sisyphus in Elysium

The rolling green meadows of Asphodel, a grass sea of prodigious mounds and mere hillocks dotted with ghostly flowers, stretched out in all directions beneath a lowering sky. A solitary figure stood at the base of the tallest rise, its crest hidden in clouds.

Thunder rumbled in the distance as Sisyphus slapped his hands together to clear the dust and grit, and then, spitting into each palm, placed them upon an enormous green boulder three times his size, smooth as glass. An eon ago, he'd named the rock Acrocorinthus, as it reminded him of the mountain that overlooked the city where he'd squandered his humanity.

He dug into the summer dirt with the balls of his feet and curling toes. He leaned into the stone's mass. His shoulder found the right spot, the muscles of his calves flexed, his thighs tightened, and his strength ran up from his legs into his back and arms.

There was a grunt that echoed over the meadow. The boulder, ever so slightly, broke its deal with gravity, inching forward, barely any distance at all, and rolling back from the incline. Sisyphus rocked his burden to-and-fro ten times, slowly building momentum. He screamed like a wounded animal, and then, drooling, legs quivering, sweat upon his brow, he slowly ascended.

The condition of the ground was good, but rain was coming, lurking just somewhere over the next few crests. He challenged himself to make it to the top before the grass got slick and the ground turned to mud. Every iota of distance he won was an enormous strain. With muscles and joints burning, in intimate contact with the smooth surface of his personal tribulation, he needed to concentrate.

For the past millennium, at this juncture, he always returned to the same episode in his life. He'd thought through it 72 million different ways and would certainly think through it again. It took over his mind, letting his chest and biceps contend with the agony.

The time he cheated death happened back in the city of Ephyra, where he had ruled neither wisely nor well. He was a shrewd and conniving character, and the gods took a disliking to him. Treachery was afoot in his court; it was no secret to him. Zeus worked his cosmic will against the king of Ephyra to little avail. Sisyphus had outsmarted the gods more than once, and once was unforgiveable.

Before he was assassinated, he told his wife, Merope, that when he died, she was to throw his naked body into the street at the center of town. She complied with his wishes, as he knew she would, and because he'd not been buried, he was cast away onto the shores of the river Styx, forever unable to cross over into the afterlife.

Upon those sorrowful shores, he sought out Persephone, goddess of spring, on her yearly, contractual visit to Hades. When he tracked her down, just as she was stepping upon Charon's boat to make the trip across the wild water, he laid out his case to her that he should be sent back to the world above in order to reprimand his wife and arrange for a burial for himself. With these tasks accomplished, he swore he would return to be judged.

The fair goddess, innocent as the season she represented, granted his wish. Of course, once he regained life, he didn't return to the realm of the dead but resumed his role as monarch of Ephyra and was soon up to his old tricks, betraying the secrets of Athena and plotting his brother's murder by poison. Eventually the gods had to send Hermes to fetch him back to the afterlife.

He stumbled in a rut and in an instant the boulder turned on him. It took him to the limits of his strength to wrestle the green globe into submission. His success cheered him, and he pushed on, breathing harder now. The rock grew heavier with every step. He whispered his queen's name, *Merope,* repeating it like a prayer, struggling to remember her affection and a time he was worthy of it. Sometimes he'd look up and see his reflection in the glassy surface of his work and it often spoke to him of things he dared not tell himself.

The rains came and went, the scorching heat of summer, snow and ice, circling for a hundred years. Then one day he was there at the crest of the hill, and he was no longer pushing the boulder but leaning against it to prop himself up. His body made haunted noises as the muscles and tendons relaxed. He took a deep breath and staggered away from his charge.

A minute, think of it as a century, passed, and as always, the enormous rock somehow rolled to the edge of the hill. A moment later it tipped forward and then was off, galloping down the slope like a charging beast and quickly disappearing into the cloud cover. In his imagination, he saw Acrocorinthus already waiting for him at the bottom.

He descended along the path the boulder had made. During journeys to be reunited with the rock, his mind wandered, and he wondered how his life and death might have been different. He often thought of one summer day out behind their cottage, in a clearing in the tall grass—yellow butterflies, white clouds, blue sky—as the young Merope, copper hair and green eyes, discovered his future in the palm of his hand. She promised to follow him in his ascent to the throne of Corinth.

It had taken mere centuries of pushing the stone before he realized that only the intangible things in life had been worthy of pursuit—love, friends, laughter, hope. Instead, during his years above, he'd chosen to value wealth and contracted greed, which swept him up into its tempest. Soon murder made sense, treachery was second nature, and lies were the meat of his meal. The boulder was a strict teacher, though, and through the torrent of hours, he reversed all his burning compulsions for material wealth, grew calm with his work, and saw he'd been a fool in his life.

The work of the boulder was simple, impossible work. When he strained beneath its weight, grappling for purchase against the incline, time disappeared. He was lost to the task at hand. At first, he considered his sentence a crushing labor, but on and on through the eons he'd come to realize it was hardly work at all and more a necessary form of meditation. His wildest dream from deep in those contemplations was that if he continued on with his work into infinity, somewhere along that misty track he would, himself, become a god through the mere process of repetition.

The planets swung in their arcs, and before too many years, he reached a spot on the hill where he could look out across the meadow, and also down to where the boulder sat like a fly spec amidst the green grass and white flowers. Suspended from the rock ceiling of the underworld was an iron gray cloud that stretched above everything. First the rain came, falling cool and soft on the hillside. Then, a tearing sound, like a shriek, and a sizzling bolt of lightning streaked down from above.

As if the dart had been hurled by an accurate hand, it pinpointed and struck the flyspeck below. The boulder shattered into pebbles, and green dust flew everywhere. He blinked and looked again, and it was still vanished. The air rushed out of him and he fell to his knees. He looked over each shoulder for angry gods and tried to swallow the agony of having his work obliterated.

Fighting through a great fear, of what he wasn't sure, he got to his feet and staggered down the path. For the longest time, he waited there at the base of the hill where the boulder had nestled, expecting his tormentors to provide a new one. Nothing arrived. Eventually, he could sit still no longer and his memory of exertion demanded he move. He walked the meadow, up and down hills, pretending to push an invisible boulder. The enterprise was all unsatisfactory and disturbing.

Time scattered like dust and he finally settled into the routine. He came to realize that the vistas were astonishing on the rare days the sun showed itself underground. Slowly, the absence of work soaked in and he even began to remember how to sleep. On the night that he realized there wouldn't be another boulder, he made a tea of the roots of the white flowers and drank it. He was now on his own, and although he missed the embrace of the smooth rock, the next morning he set out walking toward the west. Having tried all four directions, it was the one he favored.

Think of the years like leaves in autumn, and that's how many he traveled. He'd learned to sleep on his feet, and it allowed him to walk through the long nights and deep into the heart of the west. He suffered loneliness, a longing not only for Acrocorinthus but those unseen gods who had overseen his punishment. After many a summer, the light from an oasis in the distance woke him from a dream of Merope singing an enchantment to their first child, and he found himself upon a long thoroughfare leading to its gates.

Those gates were unguarded, and he entered onto the shaded path that cut beneath tall ancient trees hung with moss. The peacocks scurried before him, and goldfinches swooped and darted. He found a pond along the path with a crude wooden bench placed before it. Sisyphus sat and stared into the water, watching the orange fishes swim. A young girl ran by. He called to her, "Where is this?" and she replied without slowing, "Elysium."

The place was enchanted with apparitions and alluring scents. It was a land of Whim. If he desired a drink, a drink would appear in his hand; along with it a keg of wine and an entire party of friendly revelers to help him celebrate. The women he conjured were beautiful, unique. There were books in the libraries of Elysium recorded from Homer's memory that had never been born into the world.

Sisyphus shook off the peculiarities of death in the color, music, and swirling laughter of Elysium. Within its confines, he could adjust the pace of time from a dizzying rush to a crawl. The evenings lasted all season long and were filled with parties and assignations, games of hide and seek down long columned halls of an ancient architecture. Every moment brimmed with wonder. For a brief respite from that charmed life, he returned to the pond he'd first encountered the day he arrived, and let the spirit of place seep into him. There was something in the air and water of Elysium that made him forget for whole minutes at a time the hill and the rock and the struggle.

One afternoon, as he approached his sacred spot, he found someone sitting on the bench. It appeared to be a woman, wrapped in pale blue material, her head dimly glowing, her scent the very same as the advent of winter across the meadow. At first, he was going to fly away to the wine garden (yes, in Elysium he could fly), but instead he stayed and approached her. She looked up at him, and he felt for a moment an agony greater than the boulder ever offered.

"Merope," he whispered.

She put her finger to her lips, and when he lunged to take her in his arms, she backed away, wearing a scared expression.

"No, no," he said. "I've changed."

Still she shrunk from him. "How?"

"The stone has changed me. I pushed the weight of my misdeeds up a tall hill. Again and again."

"It must have been a gigantic boulder," she said.

"One's deeds are the only thing heavier than one's heart in the underworld."

"Trust me, I know," said Merope.

"You loved me in our early years together, didn't you?"

She nodded. "They're the most distant memories of all."

"I'll find you," he said.

She held out her arms and they embraced. As he pressed himself to her, she faded to smoke and drifted out over the water. He rose, went to the edge of the pond, and looked for her in its depth. The fish swam through his reflection, bobbing up with open mouths to catch and swallow his tears.

Later that afternoon, he did fly to the wine garden and stayed there for a long time into the night, imbibing to excess and beyond in the presence of Cronus, the Titan King of Elysium. The old man was fierce, with a lot of teeth, and wore an expression of dangerous stupidity. It was said he'd eaten his children to save himself and before being made king of Elysium his son Zeus had thrown him into Tartarus, the lowest reaches of the afterlife, devoid of light, for many many years. "The gods have instructed me to keep an eye on you," he said.

The only aspect of himself he could remember as he flitted here and there was a vague sensation of the weight of the rock against his palms. He missed the heft of it, the strategy of steering its colossal mass up the treacherous hill. It had been an anchor for him, a center to the startling afterlife that was all drift and nightmare. His ascent and descent were a ritual that brought order to the infinite. In an afternoon's conversation with the apparition of Sophocles, he discussed the frantic spinning sleep of Paradise. Think of the minutes swarming like gnats on a long, hot day. At the sudden end of the conversation, as Sisyphus fell toward sleep, the philosopher suggested, "In Elysium you can live your own story."

When he woke, he turned his back on the whirlwind, the endless drinking, the flying here and there. Instead he used all his imagination and powers of concentration, all his desire, to conjure an image of Merope and a cottage in the country for them to live in. It was remarkable how near to the woman in life his apparition came. Her copper hair and green eyes were so perfect they startled him with his own power of memory.

She was lovely, dressed in flowing gowns and bedecked with emeralds. She drifted through the days in calm silence. And when he spoke to her, he could tell she was really listening to his every word. He spoke at length about his dreams in Elysium, all his personal philosophy he'd accrued in his centuries pushing the rock. He went on and on, and she never blinked. In bed, her every move intuited his desire.

His constant attention on himself left the charade of love somewhat threadbare. So he asked her what had happened to her after Hermes had come and spirited him away and he died a second time. She seemed taken aback by the question, stuttering to speak but unable to get anything out. "Tell me anything you can remember," he said to comfort her. Still she couldn't produce a single word. Eventually he blurted out, "Then tell me how you died."

"How?" she asked.

In the same moment he wondered if she'd been assassinated by his brother, she spoke the words, "I was assassinated by your brother." The story poured forth from her in all its expected intrigue. It was in those moments, while she told of her poor fate, that Sisyphus realized the Merope he'd conjured could never be anything other or more than the product of his imagination.

He felt as though he was slipping more surely than if he'd hit an ice patch on the slope and the boulder was quick to teach him a lesson. At that moment, there was a knocking. Merope had huddled into herself, eyes closed, and she said nothing. Sisyphus opened the door. It was the Titan, Cronus, King of Elysium. He had to bend low in order to enter the cottage.

"She'll torment you no more," said the king. He pushed past Sisyphus, walked straight to Merope, and took her wrist in his hand. From the moment he touched her, she became increasingly vague and began drifting away at the edges.

"What are you doing to her?"

"I'm erasing her memory from you. Orders from the gods. You're to think of her no more. If you forget her, you can stay in Elysium."

The disintegrating Merope suddenly reached toward Sisyphus with her free hand, and he heard her cry out as if from a nightmare. The sound of it moved him and he ran at Cronus, engaging him in a struggle. He wrapped his rock-callused hands around the king's throat and squeezed. The old man punched his cheek with a fist like a mace, and a tooth flew from his mouth. It was followed by another hammer blow from the opposite side. Still, Sisyphus leaned into the battle and used his great strength to force Cronus back. He shouted for Merope to escape.

The brawl moved on, inching uphill, a trading of blows, a choking session, a wrestling match to end all matches. The cottage disappeared from around them in a strong wind, flying away piece by piece. The grass was covered with frost, and sleet fell across the hill. Cronus had the upper hand for a time, and then Sisyphus would counter and be in charge, until the day it became clear that the old god had at some point become the boulder, Acrocorinthus.

As he strained beneath the weight of his task, Sisyphus happened to see his reflection in the sheen of the boulder. The likeness opened its mouth and said, "You never cared about Merope. She didn't even have copper hair and green eyes. All you knew of her love was to take it and throw it away. She despised you and planned your assassination." With these words, his conjured image of Merope, his false knowledge of Merope, fell back into the dark recesses of his memory. Pushing the boulder with all his might, he scrabbled to leave the cold, empty loss of her.

The solitary journey ahead took forever. The hill he now ascended was steeper and more difficult than the one before he'd gone to Elysium. There were forests and lakes and a decade of loose scree, ten centuries of rain, an indefinite duration of wavering concentration. The story of how he cheated death no longer did the trick. The merest inkling of a false Merope made him shudder. Her absence was a ghost in the cottage that was his head, a current of cold air between his ears that nearly froze his effort.

It came on slowly. With the awareness of a child in the dark, he felt the sodden spirit creeping through his limbs, and the rock became more insistent. He summoned his strength, found it asleep, and wondered if he was vanishing into the infinite. At that moment his knees buckled, his biceps failed, his Achilles tendons screamed. His work slipped from his hands and dashed away down the hill, splintering tall pines in its fierce descent.

It had never happened before that he hadn't gotten the rock to the top of the hill. He feared Zeus's thunderbolts as punishment for his failure. There was nothing, though—complete silence, total stillness. It was a mild night on the meadow of Asphodel, halfway up the tallest hill within sight. He spat and fought his lethargy in order to follow the trail of the boulder down into the forest and beyond.

It wasn't long before he realized that the woods around him had gone completely black. He couldn't see and kept his hands out in front of him to avoid tree trunks. More than once he smashed his shins against a fallen log or twisted an ankle in a rut. There were no stars nor moon in the underworld, although when he pictured Acrocorinthus, sitting alone where ever it was, he pictured it gleaming in the moonlight.

He was on the verge of collapse from his final exertions against the boulder. The only thing that kept him from falling to the ground was the feel of a small hand in the center of his palm. He closed his fingers around it. It gently but confidently pulled him forward into the darkness. A soft voice spoke to him from just below his ear.

"Tell me, stranger, what is your punishment in the underworld?"

"I am the murderous, thieving king of Ephyra and am forced to push the weight of my earthly transgressions up a steep hill for eternity. I'm looking for a large green boulder that might have crashed through here this evening."

"No boulders and no evening. Follow me and I'll explain."

Her presence next to him brought him energy and excitement. He'd not felt another's touch in half the age of the cosmos.

"You are Sisyphus, bane of the gods," she said.

"My name precedes me," he said and noticed that they now seemed to be floating along above the ground rather than walking. It made for an uneasy feeling in the total dark, not knowing what's up or down.

"I'm your wife, Merope. It was so long ago. Do you remember?"

"Yes."

She spoke and he listened to her voice and saw in his imagination for the first time since death the true face of Merope—wide eyes and short black hair. "I too have been serving out my punishment in the underworld. I led many people to their doom in life and have been treated to a taste of eternity."

"After all these millennia, I finally have found my way back to you. For the longest time I couldn't remember you but only the memory of not remembering. Your touch," he said and reached around her with his free arm. He encountered nothing although he still felt her hand in his. They continued on through the darkness. He didn't sense the forest around him any longer.

She told him a memory she had from when they had lived together. A night outside in the field next to their place, drinking wine and dancing around a fire. "I asked you if you loved me and you said, 'More than anything.'"

The memory came back to him with the speed of a boulder descending. "Yes, I see it," he said. "It was from before I was king and you were queen."

"When did that feeling end?" she wondered.

They discussed it as they floated away into the dark. He apologized; she considered it. Time went by and she told him of all she'd accomplished acquiring wealth and power in his absence. He laughed and told her about Elysium.

"I've heard of it," she said.

The further they descended into nothing, the simpler the memories became. He told her that somewhere in eternity he realized he'd loved her. "Did you ever have any feelings for me?" he asked.

"I did," she said but what came after that was complicated. She laid out her explanations and recriminations gracefully, although some of it cut him hard. She told him that her punishment had been assigned by Zeus and it was to lure men and women into the deep heart of Tartarus from which nothing returns. Upon hearing this, Sisyphus clutched her hand more firmly. "Stay with me till then," he said and she promised she would.

The Jeweled Wren

On a late October afternoon, the sun still casting a weak warmth, Gary, 65, a large man with a drastic crew cut, and Hester, 62, a small woman with big glasses and short gray hair, sat out behind the garden on the green plastic bench drinking bourbon, taking in the autumn wind, and looking out across the stubbled wheat field toward a house a half-mile distant.

They talked about their daughters, grown up and moved away, how the cut field looked like a Brueghel painting, Hester's uncertainty about the woman at work who would soon replace her when she retired. After that burst of conversation there was silence.

Gary finally broke it a few minutes later, saying, "So, did we ever decide what the fuck is going on over at that place?" He pointed with the hand holding his drink at the distant house.

She had a blue blanket wrapped around her, one corner thrown over her head like a hood. "If you notice, there's all kinds of action, but it's all subtle, incremental. And you have to be aware when you drive past."

"I noticed the hanging geranium that appears on the porch certain mornings and disappears by noon," he said.

Hester nodded. "For three weeks this past summer, I swore someone had a tomato garden going behind the place. But when I slowed down and concentrated, there was nothing there."

"Have you seen the two little blonde girls playing outside lately?"

"I haven't seen a person there in months," she said.

"There was a yellow car in the driveway when I drove past a couple of weeks ago. It was the only time I'd ever seen it there—might have been an old Mercury Topaz like we had back in the '90s."

"Never saw it," she said.

"The circumstantial evidence for being haunted kind of adds up," said Gary.

"We should go over there and look in the windows," said Hester.

"Why?"

"I have the next five days off from work, and I want to do something crazy while I still can." She poured another drink and held it up. He touched the rim of his glass to hers.

"You mean go across the field?" Gary asked.

"Now that it's cut, it'll be easy."

"With my bad leg?"

"I'll get you a cane. You've got to get up and move around anyway. That's what the doctor said about the band syndrome."

"But what if someone actually *is* living in there, and we look in the windows and they see us. We'll be fucked. Even without the bad leg, at this stage of the game, running is out of the question."

"There's nobody over there," Hester said. "The car probably belonged to a real-estate agent."

They sat drinking, watching the wind shake leaves from the giant white oak and the turkey vultures circling over the field until the sun set a little after five. Then she helped him up and as far as the garden. Eventually he got his leg going and passed beneath the apple trees on his own. Inside, she put the news on in the living room and he fed the dogs.

In bed, they talked about her retirement. He already only taught part-time at a local university. Did they really need six acres and a hundred-and-twenty-year-old home? They arrived at no answers. Luckily, the haunted house across the field wasn't mentioned. He thought that was the last he'd hear of a trip to it, but the next day she returned from Walmart with two flashlights and a cane. He asked when and she told him, "By cover of dark."

"Not tonight," he said.

She had a brief coughing spasm, the likes of which she'd been having fairly frequently of late. She nodded. Before he could complain, she caught her breath and said, "Hold on a second. Didn't you ever really want to just know what the fuck was up with something?"

"I guess," said Gary. "But . . ."

"Well, that's what's going on here. You and I, just us, together, we're going to get to the bottom of this."

"Let me see that cane," he said. He pictured himself out in the cut wheat field, lurching forward, the cane snapping beneath sudden weight and then a face-first dive into the mud.

She handed it to him and he said, "It's a cheap piece of crap. That's a cane for training horses."

"Perfect then," she said and handed him a flashlight.

The sky was clear and full of stars, but it was cold, and he felt it in his hip. Every time he leaned on the cane it sunk two inches into the damp ground and set him off balance. Still, he took a deep breath and launched himself forward into the night. She helped him along through the orchard and past the garden to the edge of the cut amber field, where she let go. He stumbled through the wheat stubble toward an old white house, invisible in the distance. Fifteen minutes later, she stood in the middle of the miles-deep field, smoking a cigarette and staring at the moon. She'd been there for nearly five minutes already, waiting for him to catch up. As he scrabbled toward her, she said, "How's the leg?"

"Hurts like a bitch," he said. "I think I feel bone on bone. This is no IT band syndrome."

"Don't give me that bone-on-bone business," she said. "Pick up the pace or we'll be at this all night."

He stopped next to her and turned to take in the enormity of the field around them. "I know why those turkey vultures were circling above here yesterday," he said. "They were feeding on the last two nitwits who decided to do something crazy."

She laughed and they walked together for a while.

From a quarter-mile distance, they could make the place out, what was left of its white paint reflecting moonlight. She strode ahead impatiently, and he hobbled over the lumpy ground. Somewhere in the middle of their approach, he had a memory of the two little girls, both in frilly white dresses, playing in a red plastic car with a yellow roof. One seemed to him a year or two older than the other.

Hester slowed down and pointed. "Check it out."

There was a dim light on in the upstairs window at the side of the house.

"Did you see it there before?" he asked. "There was no light there before, right?"

"You know, I'm not sure it's a light on inside or if it's from the moonbeams directly hitting the window. As we get closer we might find it's just a reflection."

"If there's a light on, I think we should turn back."

"We'll see," she said.

In another hundred yards, they saw it had been but a reflection, and that room was as dark as the rest.

Near the border between the field and the barnyard, Hester held up her hand to stop him. They stood in silence. She breathing heavily, he shifting his weight off the bad hip and relying on the fragile cane. There were four buildings clustered at the center of the property, all once painted white. The main house, a three-story Victorian with a wraparound porch, like their own place, a barn, a long outbuilding—a kind of garage to cover a tractor—and next to the white submarine of a propane tank, a smaller garden shed. The yard was no less than seven acres, and much of it was covered with stands of black walnut.

"Pretty quiet," whispered Gary.

"Creepy," she said.

"It doesn't get to me in a creepy way," he said. "It makes me feel like this location, right here, is so far from the rest of life it would take a week's walk along a dusty road to get within hailing distance of a Walmart."

"Where are we gonna start?" asked Hester.

"I don't care, but no breaking and entering."

"The garden shed is probably bullshit," she said. "The tractor garage, I can tell right now there's nothing in it." She turned her flashlight beam on the structure's opening and the light shone straight through into a stand of trees on the other side. "The barn is interesting but it looks locked up. Let's start with the house."

"I don't care," he said. "The place is dead. We're too late."

"Cheer up," she said and crossed the boundary onto the lawn.

He followed her, and immediately it was a relief to be able to walk on flat ground and not up and down the furrowed muddy plough rows complicated by what remained of the shorn wheat. They passed the oak whose biggest branch held a tire swing. The half-deflated tube turned in the wind.

"Maybe we should sneak around a little first and see if we hear anybody inside."

"OK," she said and instead went straight around to the front of the house, stepped up to the parlor windows, turned on the flashlight, and pressed her face to the glass.

When he caught up with her, he stood behind her, off the porch. "What do you see?" he asked.

"There's furniture and stuff in there."

"So they never moved out?" he said.

"Unless maybe they just left everything and fled."

"But they couldn't have, because we saw them here as late as February, and I know I saw the girls one day in spring. Remember in March when it snowed eight inches? They had a sled out in the yard and were pushing each other around."

"I'd seen the mother there quite a few times for a while."

"Young woman, short blond hair."

Hester nodded. She turned away from the window. "Did you ever actually see her face?" She walked to the edge of the porch and he took her hand as she descended the steps. They headed around the house to search for other windows.

"Now that you mention it, no. I never saw her face," he said. "What about the guy, did you ever see his face?"

"No."

"I remember that guy always had on a plain white T-shirt. Plain white T-shirt and jeans," said Gary.

Along the side of the house, in the shadows near the chimney, she spotted, without use of the flashlight, a little set of steps that descended to a basement entrance. The door to the basement had glass panes, still intact, and a glint of starlight caught her eyes. She stopped, backtracked, and only as she took the concrete stairs, flipping on her light, did Gary realize where she was headed. He watched from ground level as she descended.

"Well?" he said.

"I have news for you," she called over her shoulder. "This door's unlocked."

Then he heard the screeching of the hinges as she pushed through the opening and stepped inside. He turned on his flashlight for the first time and gingerly descended, keeping one arm pressed against the side of the house and using the cane with every placement of his right foot. She'd left the door open, and he could see her light beam jumping around the pitch-black room.

The place smelled of damp and dirt; it was colder inside than it had been in the autumn field. The vault held one skid with boxes of what looked to be Christmas decorations, wilted silver garland spilling out the top. Another few boxes, also on skids, but those closed up and stacked neatly. There was the propane heater, the water softener, the fuse box mounted on the wall. A toad leaped across the dirt floor, heading for the shadows.

"At every corner of the basement," said Hester, "there's a plate with a rotting horse chestnut on it. Could be some ghost nonsense."

"It's to keep spiders out of the house," said Gary.

"How do you know that?" she asked.

"Some guy told me when I was over walking in the preserve. There are a couple of those trees and they'd dropped these weird green globes. I asked the guy what they were and he told me all about them and the thing about the spiders. I asked him if the spider thing really worked. He said, 'Good as anything.'"

"Now what?" she asked. "There's the stairs up into the house." She pointed with her flashlight beam.

"Come on," he said. "What are we even looking for anyway?"

"Anything ghost-like or ghost related"

"Let's go home," he said.

She shushed him and started up the stairs.

In the kitchen, they found dishes in the sink, and a cigarette ash as long as a cigarette on the counter. Someone, some months back, left behind a cup of coffee and an English muffin with two small bites out of it. She opened the refrigerator. No light shone out, but a smell like Death itself wafted through the room.

She slammed the door closed. "Bad meat," she whispered. "The power's off to everything."

"God, that smell. Maggots in my brain from it."

She'd already moved on and was inspecting the cabinets. "Look here," she quietly called to him. Her flashlight illuminated the contents of a cupboard. "What do you see there?"

He moved closer and added the glow of his own flashlight. "Six cans of Beefaroni and a withered potato sprouting eyes."

"I'd say that's at least tangentially haunted."

"Does six cans mean they liked it or they didn't?" he asked.

From the kitchen, they moved on to the second floor, where there were three bedrooms. He complained in whispers throughout his awkward ascent, the flimsy cane without a rubber tip tapping loudly upon each step.

"Keep it down," she said as he hobbled up next to her in the hallway of bedrooms. It was clear right away from the thumb-tacked drawings on the doors that each of the girls had their own room.

He surmised that the one at the far end of the hallway from the stairs belonged to the parents.

"Pick one," she said. "We'll just look in and take a peek and then we'll split. The place smells like ancient ass."

"No argument there," said Gary.

She took the left-hand side and he the right. They pushed open their respective sister's doors, flashlights lit and ready.

Hester rummaged for only moments before discovering some pages of homework scattered upon the dresser. There she read her charge's name—Imsa Bridges. The girl's handwriting was very neat. Her theme was the four seasons. In it she claimed that the last days of summer might be the most beautiful of all. She likened winter to a sleep, and the autumn, heralded by the wind chime, was a season in which secrets both hideous and bright were revealed. Of spring, there was no mention.

In Gary's room, there was a hole in the middle pane of the triple-paned window. It looked as if the glass had been suddenly punched out. Rain had invaded and puddled on the floor. The dampness, the cold, brought fog with each breath and made his teeth chatter. As he moved his flashlight around, he saw that shelves of a fine blue fungus had grown all over the walls. From outside there came a noise of tires on gravel, and in that instant he looked down and there was a picture frame holding a faded Polaroid of one of the girls. The frame was made of blocks with letters, and the letters spelled her name, "Sami Bridges."

"Shit," he heard Hester say across the hall. He hobbled toward her door, and as he did she came out and whispered, "Turn off the flashlight."

"What?"

"Someone just pulled up in an old yellow car."

"Fuck," he said, and with that word they heard the front door downstairs creak open. She took him by the arm, and they moved along the hallway toward the last room. She whispered to him as they went, "If I hear that fuckin' cane on the floor, I'm gonna beat ya with it."

From downstairs came a bellowing male voice, "Sunny?"

The next thing Gary knew he was on his considerable stomach on the floor and Hester was shoving while he shimmied under the bed. After he was hidden, she tiptoed around to the other side and got under. Once she was in place they found each other's hands to hold.

"This is so fucked up," he whispered.

"Shhh."

The voice called again, this time up the stairs from the first floor. "Sunny?" There were footsteps ascending. As if that started something in motion up on the third floor, they heard the screams of children and a woman repeating the phrase "Save yourself."

The door opened. Somehow the electricity had come back on, because light from the hallway streamed in. From where they lay, they could see the boots, the jeans, and the bottom of the intruder's white T-shirt. They watched him open the middle drawer of a dresser and reach in. When his hand reappeared, it was holding a revolver. He left the room and a moment later they heard him on the stairway to the third floor.

"Hurry up," she whispered and slipped out from under the bed. She ran to his side, grabbed his arm, and pulled harder than he pushed to free him. The first gunshot upstairs went off as they clasped hands and she helped him to his feet. Before the second shot went off they'd reached the stairs. Gary was moving faster than he knew he could. The pain was there but its importance paled in relation to the promise of gunplay. When Hester opened the front door, deep screams of agony rained down from above.

Gary went through the door left open by Hester but didn't count on the screen door that came back hard and clipped him on his left shoulder. It left him off balance when he went to take the first step down off the porch. His leg on the side of the bad hip just suddenly gave out, as it occasionally did, and by the time he reached the yard he was staggering toward a fall, madly employing unsuccessful cane work until his face was in the mud.

Hester helped her husband to his feet and brushed him off. He looked around on the ground for the cane and saw it by moonlight in two pieces. "Why aren't we running?" he asked her.

"Look," she said and they turned around. "The car is gone and the house is perfectly quiet."

"Well, we certainly got to the bottom of that," he said.

She took his arm around her shoulders and he leaned a little on her with each step as they made their way back across the field.

Despite how cold it had gotten, and that their words were steam, they sat on the porch, low music, three candles burning, bourbon and ice. He leaned back in his rocker and said, "So what'd you make of it?"

"You think he killed them all and then himself?" she said.

"Or they all killed him, or the girls killed the folks, or the wife did them all. Or just maybe, nobody killed anybody."

"Yeah," she said. "The whole thing seemed kind of melodramatic. Did it ring true to you?"

He shrugged. "All I can say is I was scared shitless. What about you?"

"I'm not sure I even saw what I saw," she said.

"Some of it's vague," he admitted. "Could have been like a communal hysterical dream between the two of us."

"After we got outside, and you took a dive . . ." She raised her eyebrows and stifled a laugh.

"I told you that cane was for shit."

"Anyway," she continued, "before I picked you up, I saw something hanging on the branch of a pear tree right in the front of the house. By then I realized the car and its driver had vanished.

Before I came to pick you up, I stuffed this thing in my jacket as a souvenir." She took off her glove and reached into her pocket. Slowly, she brought forth something made of bright metal. She laid it on the table between them, and he lit it with his flashlight.

There were jewels—fake or real, he couldn't tell—in red, green, and blue. It was a bird in a nest feeding its chicks. Beneath hung metal chimes on thick wire. "It's a wren, I think," she said. She picked it up off the small table and stood. Leaning off the porch, she hung the wind chime on a branch of an ornamental maple only an arm's length away. Before returning to her seat, she ran her fingers along the bottoms of the chimes and they sounded like icicles colliding. She shivered and pulled the blanket wrapped around her over her shoulders. The wind picked up and the temperature dropped.

"Harassing the nest of a wren in Eurasia is bad luck," he said.

"How do you come up with this bullshit?" she asked.

"I must have read it somewhere."

They had another drink and spent the next hour talking themselves out of the experience they'd had at the Bridges house. Eventually they sat in silence and soon after fell asleep wrapped up against the cold and fortified with bourbon. The sound of the wind chime in their dreams was like children giggling. A little before 4:00 a.m, he woke her and they went inside and up the stairs to bed.

Beginning the next day, there was an unspoken understanding between them not to bring the Bridges house up in conversation. When Gary went out to teach, he went the long way around so as not to pass the place. Only across the empty winter field, a dot in the distance on the brightest day, an impression of sorrow on a cloudy one, would he deign to view the Bridges house. Hester also avoided passing the place, and drove the five miles out to the highway no matter where she was going.

Past harvest to the first snow, Gary left the window open in his office. He counted on the cool air to keep him awake while he wrote. All through those days as the last frayed threads of summer vanished and the world turned toward darkness, the jeweled wren sounded, its intermittent tinkling ever a surprise. Its music leaked in through his office window while he worked and swamped his thoughts. Sometimes when he'd stopped typing and was staring at the wall, the two blonde girls came back to him. And from some distant recesses of his memory came a voice bellowing, "Sunny?"

Hester sat out on the covered porch every night, no matter the weather. Fierce winds, frozen temperatures, blowing snow never stopped her. She put on her parka, cocooned herself in a blanket, and took her bourbon outside to smoke and cough or both. There were nights when Gary joined her, but often she sat by herself and decompressed from the day at work, inspecting and then consciously forgetting each incident from the office she ran. One night in early November, she heard a sound like angels whispering, and when she realized it was the chimes, she smiled and wept.

They spent Thanksgiving together, eating dinner at the Uncertain Diner. Later there were drinks on the porch. She smoked and he fiddled with a music box he'd recently bought where through Bluetooth you could listen to the music from your phone. Three bourbons in, Gary's favorite head music swirled the night. Hester said, "We've got to go back."

At first he said nothing, but eventually he nodded and said, "I can't believe I'm saying this, but yeah."

"Tonight," she told him.

"One stipulation," he said. "Let's take the fucking car."

"There are no other houses over there, and once you're off the road, it's so dark no one will see. I can park it in the empty tractor shed and we can walk from there."

"Solid."

"Above all others, what's the one thing you want to know?" she asked.

"I'll start with a general what the fuck and proceed from there."

"I want to know the calamity of events that led to it."

"Led to what?"

"Whatever tragedy keeps calling these people back."

"Jeez," he said and poured them each another drink.

Hester drove Gary's CRV. They rounded the corner and as the Bridges place drew near, she turned out the headlights and coasted through the dark. She slowly piloted the car in and around tree trunks and hid it in the old structure as she'd said she would. Gary had a better cane, stronger, made to support the weight of an adult. It had a rubber tip and grips along the crook. His hip was worse every day, and walking was becoming too great an effort, but Hester insisted he keep moving. So he did. They both wore all black and carried their flashlights. She brought the taser she'd bought online. He'd asked why she didn't just buy a gun. And she said, "I don't want to kill anyone."

"How do you kill a ghost?" said Gary.

"You know what I mean."

She led him through the shadows and he tried mightily to keep up with her. From using the cane, he'd adopted a rocking, side-to-side gait like he was a windup toy. The house loomed in front of them and they slipped around the side to where the steps led down. They took the same route as they had before. This time they didn't inspect the basement but went straight for the stairs that led up into the house. They passed the refrigerator and the Chef Boyardee and went directly to the hallway on the second floor.

"Same rooms?" he asked.

"No, up to the third floor."

"We'll be trapped up there."

"We have to get up there and hide before that whole thing goes down."

"Hide?"

"Yeah, so we see what happened. We need to know more."

He shook his head but followed her up the steps, which led to a large room, a window on every wall. It was lined with carpets and plush furniture in a powder blue with silver trim that shimmered in the flashlights' glare.

"Find a place to hide," she said.

He turned in a circle, looking for something substantial to hide behind where it wouldn't discomfort his hip, but there wasn't anything that big in the room. "I'm not getting on the floor again."

"Shhh. Go in the closet over there," said Hester and pointed with the light beam.

He saw where she meant, went to it and opened the door. It was dark and empty, damp concrete. *Who has a concrete closet?* he thought. He stepped in and closed the door behind him but didn't shut it. When he got in position, leaning on his cane, he peered out and around the room, using the flashlight, and finally found her ducked behind a sewing machine on a wooden box in the corner. The instant he spotted her, he heard tires on gravel. A moment after he doused his light, the front door downstairs flung open and that voice called, "Sunny!"

The lights came on at once in a silent explosion. And there were the mother and two girls sitting on couches. The girls were silent and stock-still in their white party dresses. From Gary's vantage point in the closet, he stood behind and above the blond woman who sat on a divan in front of him. He watched her turn around on her seat. She had only eyes that stared directly into the sliver of an opening he watched through and pierced his gaze. "Save yourself," she said as if directly to him. That's when Mr. Bridges stepped through the door, head turned in a way that made it impossible for Gary or Hester to clearly see his face.

He wasn't in the door more than a moment before she again said, "Save yourself."

As he approached his wife, the two girls slid off the bench they were sitting on and fell to their knees. They clasped hands in prayer and recited the Act of Contrition. While they prayed, a dark cloud began to form against the wall across the room. They prayed hard, in unison, eyes peering through the roof to heaven. The father lifted the gun and put it inches from the back of the older girl's head.

It became obvious that the intonation of their words was the impetus for the cloud to take the shape of a man in a raincoat and hat. The vagueness of smog solidified into a cruel face, sharp like an axe head but also handsome. He walked forward as in a slow dream and took the gun from Mr. Bridges' hand. Hester thought she heard cymbals clash, and next she knew, the husband and wife were bleeding profusely from a hundred cuts each. The fog man moved with such speed and grace she didn't see the blade until he was almost done filleting them. Seven more stabs between them and the mother and father fell to the floor in puddles of blood.

He called for the girls, still praying, to follow him. They stood in silence and did as they were told. As they headed for the door, Hester and Gary saw that, at his edges, the man in coat and hat was beginning to transform, vines of smoke slowly twining upward. Just then a coughing fit seized her. The fog fellow stopped, spun around on his heels, and took in the parlor. Gary didn't watch, but he heard the words, "You, in the corner. Come out of there." His legs went numb and his breathing became erratic. There was a struggle, and the stranger bellowed, "Come with me for a drive." Gary could tell Hester was being dragged toward the stairs.

He lunged out of the closet as the sisters passed, knocking them over like pins in a split, his cane waving in the air. He clutched it near the rubber tip and swung the crook end at the head of the abductor. Hester reached into her jacket pocket and took out the taser. She pressed the button to charge it up and then jammed it against the fog man's rippling neck. He was solid and smoke at the same time. With the addition of the electricity, his head lit up and he glowed green like an iridescent fish. The application of the cane nearly knocked him down. He staggered and Hester broke free of his grip.

Gary caught her in his arms. She turned and screamed, "Get out!" at the ghosts.

The man in the raincoat and hat turned to dust, and each of the sisters became a puddle. The lights were out and he was suddenly hard pressed to remember an instance where they hadn't been all night.

"I'm never coming back here," Hester said, as much to the walls as to Gary. "It's a trap."

He said nothing until they were driving through the snow. "It'd take us a hundred trips to figure the whole thing out."

"I don't want it anymore," she said. "I don't want to know. I'm too tired."

Gary and Hester tried to forget the entire enterprise, but the sound of the chime on the porch had the ability to drill through the walls of the house and find them wherever they were. Every time the wind blew that winter they contemplated the mystery, extrapolating scenarios based on the flimsy knowledge they'd gathered. By January, they were aware that every sounding of the wind chime distorted Time, lengthening seconds, shrinking weeks, twisting speed and dealing crooked minutes. A year buzzed by like a mosquito and they were retired.

Hours became epics, and Gary and Hester missed each other, passing along different corridors. Whole days went by and he wouldn't see her, but he heard her above or below in the house and could call out and she would answer him. He would call that he loved her and she would answer the same. Different seasons, all but spring, came and went. And eventually her presence grew rarer and her voice quieter. One weak cough from some far-flung room of the old house. The sudden noise of a toilet flushing downstairs or the microwave dinging woke him from sleep in the middle of the night. These intermittent sounds, proof she was still there, helped him hold out hope that he'd run into her before long. Eventually, though, they stopped altogether, along with the written notes she'd leave through her days like breadcrumbs on the trail. The loneliness overwhelmed him.

One afternoon, he found himself in the bedroom, unable to recall why he was there. He happened to look out the window and saw her standing in the driveway with two suitcases. She wore her beret she only put on when traveling. He couldn't believe it was her and tried to lift the window to call out for her to wait for him. His hip was so bad that by the time he reached the side door and the driveway, she was gone. He caught a glimpse of the yellow car, turning out into the street and heading away. He staggered, about to fall, and the blond girls appeared on either side of him. They helped him into his rocker on the porch, pulled down the shade of night, and set the breeze to blowing.

"Where's he taking Hester?" asked Gary. "The man with the raincoat and hat. Where?"

"Shhh," said Imsa. "Every ghost story is your own."

"Where's he taking her?" he repeated.

"To find out," said Sami, and their high, light laughter became the music of the jeweled wren.

Not Without Mercy

The snow angled down fiercely out of the west, filling the parking lot and road and fields beyond. Amy stood at the office window and peered into the storm, trying to spot the headlights of Harry's old truck coming up Sossey Road. She shut off the lamps and signs out by the pumps in order to see better. Her boss, Fareed, had called earlier and told her not to shut down the gas in case someone traveling through the storm might need fuel. "Cash, they're out of luck," he'd said. "But a debit card, yes. Travelers in need." He'd laughed and so had she, but now she was worried. It was a ten-mile drive from the edge of town out to the gas station and it looked to her like there was already eight inches on the ground, no sign of letup. Drifts were forming in the road.

She took out her cell phone and dialed Harry. Three rings later, he answered. "Have you left yet?" she asked. "I was just thinking I could stay here on the cot and you could come out tomorrow morning and get me. It looks really shitty out there."

"Too late," said Harry. "I'm here."

She peered again and now saw the headlights and the silhouette of falling snow they cast. "OK," she said and hung up.

Harry pulled into the darkened parking lot. Amy put her coat on and locked the garage and office doors. She left the office light on as a gesture to lonely passersby. He stayed in the truck and rolled his window down as she approached.

"How's Sossey?" she asked.

"Bad. We'll have to take it slow and hope we don't get stuck."

She walked around to the passenger side of the truck, clasping closed the top of her coat with her right hand. The door of the truck squealed miserably and she shook her head. "How old is this rolling pile?"

"Shhh," he said, patted the dashboard, and then lit the two cigarettes he held between his lips. She got situated in the seat, shut the door, and he handed her one.

"How are the kids?" she asked and took a long drag, closing her eyes like she was praying.

"They're in bed, asleep. Your old man is listening for them."

"Good," she said, and he put the truck in gear and crept out of the parking lot.

Amy tapped the pocket of her coat on the left side. "Oh, I thought I'd left it in the office."

"What?" He opened the window a slit to flick his ash.

"Fareed's wife, Susan, brought by that necklace this morning that I paid her to make for Becky. It's beautiful. Fake diamonds and a real sapphire."

"Shit, that's right, her birthday's next week."

"She's gonna be fourteen."

"Ain't that a kick in the head," said Harry, and a deafening roar pounced from above. The truck vibrated and swerved across the road. He did everything he could to keep it from going into the drainage ditch.

"What the—" said Amy, and her words were cut off by the appearance from over the truck roof of something on fire, whistling down against the storm. In a moment it was gone out of sight behind the trees. Then they heard it hit, felt it, and saw an eruption of sparks shoot up in all directions. Harry managed to keep the truck on the road and swerved around the bend ahead, which brought them closer to the field that had been brimming with soybeans not but three months earlier and now was home to whatever had dropped from the sky.

They saw the thing, the size of their garden shed, glowing in the distance. Harry slowed to a stop. "What do we do?" he asked.

"It doesn't look like a plane," said Amy.

"That's no plane."

"Is it a meteor?"

"Doesn't look like that either."

"Well, forget it," she said. "I don't want to find out."

He pushed down on the gas, the wheels spun and smoke billowed out of the exhaust pipe, but they sat pretty much where they were.

"Oh, bullshit," she said.

"Yeah." He revved the engine and spun the tires a few more times until finally she said, "OK, that's enough. Is that shovel in the back?"

"Yeah."

"I'll dig the ice out from under the tires and maybe we can grab some road." She zipped up her coat, flipped the hood on without securing it, and got out.

Harry left the lights on and kept it running. The residual glow from the high beams faintly lit the area around the sides of the truck. He found a flare in the bed, lit it, and set it up a few yards behind where they'd stopped. The wind had abated considerably since they'd left the station. Snow still came down but not quite as furiously. "I've got some sand in the back too," he said.

Amy asked him for another cigarette. He lit it in his cupped hands for her. With the butt in the corner of her lips she went to work, chipping and scraping at the frozen slush. Harry resorted to carrying handfuls of sand and throwing them under the tires.

"Hey," she said. "Let me shovel a little, otherwise I'm shoveling the sand away." She shook her head.

"Oh, sorry."

"You're an idiot," she said and they both laughed.

She dug for a while and he watched. He said, "Whatever came down in the storm has gone out. It's just dark there now."

"If it was a nicer night we could walk out and see," she said. She handed him the shovel and motioned for him to take a turn. While he went at it, she peered across the field and saw nothing but snow falling and that eventually disappearing a few yards beyond into black. She thought of that field in summer with the moon shining over it.

"I've hit road under three tires," Harry eventually called. "I'll get some sand with the shovel, throw it on there, and we'll be out of here in a minute."

"Christ, I'm freezing," said Amy.

They both heard a very odd sound coming up from the ditch at the side of the road. "Do you hear that?" he said.

"Yeah, what is it?"

"Like burbling, right?" she said.

They looked down into the ditch and something was crawling up the side of it.

"What is that?" he said.

"A possum or skunk?"

"Nah."

The thing pulled itself up the snowy embankment and stood to its full height.

"No fuckin' way," he said.

"I never saw anything like it," said Amy.

"A three-foot block of scrapple?" said Harry.

"And three tentacles."

He cocked the shovel over his shoulder, wanting to hit the thing back into the ditch, but he was stunned by the sight of it. The creature had a thousand little legs under the bottom side of that bad meat block. Those tiny legs had to scrabble like mad for it to scuttle only a half a foot. It had no eyes, just two holes at seemingly random spots on the right side of its front. One was oozing a glistening drool. The hole at the top of the left side of the body, somewhat larger than the two on the other side, poorly hid sharp teeth in a lipless hole.

Amy yelled, "Get it away."

He swung with all his might and the shovel head hit the thing with an echoing slap and thud. The blow sent it sliding down the side of the ditch. Although it sank out of sight, they could hear it still burbling and now sputtering, choking and giving off a whispered growl like a demon purring.

"What kind of deal was that?"

"Let's get out of here."

They jumped into the truck and as they shut the doors it stalled out with a shudder. She turned the key but there was only a click. Three more times she tried to start it.

"Don't flood it," he said.

"Will you shut the fuck up." She tried it again.

"The battery's brand-new," said Harry. "I just had the whole thing checked out."

"The lights are still on," she said.

"That thing's got a brain lock on us." He opened the glove compartment and pulled out a Colt pistol. "We'll see about this," he said.

As Harry was climbing back onto the road, the thing was coming up out of the ditch again. Amy jumped across the console in the middle of the seats to watch from the open passenger door. The thing waved its tentacles at Harry and advanced, albeit slowly. He raised the gun, said "Fuck you," and fired, once, twice. Harry and Amy blinked with the noise of each round. The first bullet put a neat hole through the thing, so instead of having two maybe-eye-sockets it now had three. The second shot chipped a rounded corner of scrapple off the rumbling brick of alien and brought a reedy scream from the thing. It toppled over at the edge of the incline.

Harry advanced gingerly to kick it into the ditch, only 50 percent sure it was dead. As he inched closer, one of the three tentacles popped up and, quick as a blink, shot a golden seed into his forehead. It happened too fast for Amy to see it. A moment later, one flew out and hit her in the forehead as well. He staggered backwards toward the cab of the pickup, and she reached for him from the passenger seat. They both knew the instant the golden seed entered their heads, breaking a tiny hole in the skull and burying itself in the gray matter, that they were somehow transformed. The universe whirled in his mind's eye—planets and stars and clusters, weaving in and out and around, spinning like a top. In her thoughts the ground leaped up into her through her shoes. As she reached out to touch his shoulder, the two of them turned to pink dust and blew away.

Eight minutes later, the thing was at the side of the truck. It lifted the empty clothes of Amy and Harry and inspected the pockets. In them, among other things, it found a cheap pen, the lighter, a peppermint candy stuck to the lining, a sapphire necklace. It kept the necklace and the lighter. Using its tentacles as hands, it tossed the remainder of belongings into the cab. It scuttled away through the snow, bullet wounds slowly healing beneath the action of a laving ten-inch sky-blue tongue that darted from the lipless hole in front. As it moved and healed, it inserted both the gun and the necklace into another large, lipless hole, only this one in the rear. It shoved two tentacles into two face holes and moaned low through its back hole. A second later there was an audible popping noise and the pickup vanished, snow filling the place it had been.

The creature travelled on through the night, drooling, burbling, scuttling. It moved through the storm. It moved across a field, its tracks being slowly covered, and rested in a windbreak of trees. Snow swirled around it, and it was cold. Its bottom half, dragged through every snowdrift on the way, was frigid, but the thousand legs never ceased moving. Tentacles wiggled and swooped through the air like escaped fire hoses, and it sharpened its concentration on the circle of blue within the circle of black. In among the towering white oaks, the sun now up and shining in a blue sky onto pure white, the creature found a comfortable spot and fell over, face-first.

The wind swept in among the trees and rearranged the snow to cover the gray meat package. A week later it thawed out and then proceeded to lie there beneath the trees, in the weeds, a platform for insects, a curious scent for coyotes. Seasons upon seasons passed—sun shining, rain falling, snow blowing, leaves turning. Its tentacles eventually rotted off and broke down to the point where field mice could chew them, and they did. Its thousand legs went to sod, like so many miniature cigars left out in a downpour. When the temperature climbed, gleaming liquid drizzled out and left a lavender crew-cut moss growing across the ground. The spot was so peaceful and quiet, just the wind passing through the leaves of the old trees and the padding of squirrels along the boughs.

In the midst of a very virulent spring in which the beetles made lace of leaves and yellow flowers grew throughout the thicket, there came without warning a sudden blip of air from the creature's back hole, and a mote of an idea was loosed into the atmosphere. That minuscule pink dot caught the wind and was up and out over the field in a moment. As insignificant as it seemed, it contained multitudes, the information for a command that upon contact with a human's nasal lining would download into the host to be run. The virus replaced DNA with strands of alien-spun sugar and initiated through mitochondrial transcendence in the host the conception of a story.

The virus instructed the subject to tell a long, involved tale in a certain manner, with a certain rhythm, tone, and character. In fact, the host had no choice but to perform the story for a listener the way its programmers intended. To begin listening to it meant that one couldn't stop. They became infected with it and were able to tell it exactly the same way as the initial host. When that story ran in a mind for seven days, all thoughts became irreparably corrupted and seized like a pickup engine run out of oil. The imagery of the story toppled and jumbled and choked the byways of thought till all became less and less unto nothing. Even the merest notion stalled, withered, and died.

Don't worry, this story isn't that story. The reason you know it isn't that story is because in that story Becky never got her necklace. In this story, she does. Here's how it happened.

Becky was in her mid-40s by then, married with three kids, all girls. Five nights after Christmas, she woke up around 2 a.m. to find a strange man standing at the foot of her bed, holding a lit cigarette lighter in one hand and proffering forth a sparkling necklace with the other. She cleared her eyes, believing it a dream, but there he was—a stooped old man with straggly white hair parted in the middle. He was dressed in a threadbare jacket and trousers with cigarette holes in the lap, zipper half open. She was instantly numb with fear.

The intruder leaned forward toward her from the bottom of the bed, whispering, "We are not without mercy. Take what is yours." The third time he said it, Becky nudged her husband and said, "Tim, Tim, there's someone in the room."

He pretended to still be asleep but slowly snaked his arm up the side of the nightstand and slipped his hand into the second drawer from the bottom. He got a grip on the gun and once it was firmly in his hand, he lunged upward, spun, and squeezed off five rounds. Three of them hit the old man and sent him sprawling against the closet door. One had taken out his eye, one shattered his chin, and the third was a bullseye to the Adam's apple. He slumped down into a sitting position, croaked, "Mercy," fell into a dream of the peaceful spot beneath the white oaks in the soybean field where he found the lighter and necklace the voice in his head demanded he retrieve. He fell into the lavender fuzz that spread across the ground and passed through to the next world.

The police reported the break-in at Becky and Tim's place as a burglary. A week after the medics had come and carted the old man's body away, a police officer who'd arrived that night to answer the 9-1-1 call Tim had made as the gun smoke cleared, showed up at the front door. He had the necklace and lighter and was returning them, assuming they had been stolen by the intruder that night. Becky liked the looks of the necklace so she went along with his scenario and figured she might as well get something out of the horrible incident. Tim wasn't home, which was good, because she was sure if she tried to lie to the officer in his presence, he'd have corrected her that the items weren't theirs.

Before he left, the officer told her something about the "perpetrator," as he called the burglar. "That old guy just basically disintegrated over a period of a few days. I mean a body usually sticks around till they can find relatives and bury it, but not this perp. He came apart like overcooked salmon. Just rotted away in the morgue drawer. The guys down there told me they'd never seen anything like it. Said he stank to high heaven."

"Right," said Becky, not really wanting to listen to descriptions of the demise of the horrid old pervert. The officer had more to say, but she wiggled her fingers at him in a casual goodbye and shut the front door before he could go on. That afternoon, she wore the necklace without the slightest idea it had been made specifically for her years earlier. While she sat drinking a cup of coffee, staring through the sliding glass door to the backyard, she noticed the sapphire pendant of the thing had begun to glow a deep-space indigo.

She was astonished when a blue beam shot out of the precious stone and projected a moving image on the glass door. If she could have, she'd have gotten up and run, she'd have ripped the necklace off, she'd have screamed although the house was empty. As it was, though, she was paralyzed. All she could do was watch. The scene through which she could see the white oak and the garden and shed was of a kindly looking old man with white hair and a white walrus mustache. He wore khaki pants, sandals, a V-neck sweater, powder green, with a short-sleeved white shirt under it, and he could have been the nicer brother of the man who'd broken into the house.

He sat under a tree projected upon the glass just about where the real tree could be seen through it. "Greetings," said the old man and smiled. "Call me Uncle Gribnob. I'm appearing to you in a familiar form so as not to frighten you. I'm here to offer a sort of explanation as to why your planet is being invaded and your species is being wiped out. We're not without mercy. We thought you deserved an explanation. Just keep your peace for a few minutes while I explain and then feel free to ask questions. I'll answer anything you like. Do you understand? You may nod if you do."

Becky nodded.

"OK," said the old man. "Here's the long and short of it. We take no pleasure in wiping your kind out. It's not usually our way. We're doing this for the greater good of the universe. Somebody has to do it, and since we're the most culturally and morally advanced and have the most cutting-edge technology, we've taken it upon ourselves to do the deed. Believe me, it's not without the consent, no, approval, of the other civilizations. Even the reptile people were unanimously for it.

"You see, we've all had to deal with your kind before. And what I mean by your kind is, you have a distinctive aberration in your minds that can't be healed or manipulated or fixed. And that one small mistake, that single knot in the works, so to speak, makes your species so dangerous. We've seen the results. You're not sophisticated enough yet to be a problem to the universe at large, but who wants to let things get to that point?

"Your defective brains persist to insist, with a faulty mathematics that makes your error magically vanish, that the ratio of the circumference of a circle to its diameter is an endless number. You no doubt had heard of pi in school? The ratio, in reality, is simply three, but your lack of sense dares to claim it is a number with endless decimal places. It would be funny if it weren't for what we know peoples who have this deviant pycho-structure are capable of. How can anything be endless in a limited universe? Dangerously delusional. So we're going to ease you out of existence. Questions?"

Becky could barely follow what had been said. She thought she was having a stroke or that Tim had dropped a hit of acid into her coffee before he left for work. All she managed to get out was, "What can I do?"

"Well," said Uncle Gribnob. His image wavered in and out. Finally he vanished from the glass, and she could see clearly into the backyard where the wind was blowing end of summer leaves. The necklace continued to glow and his voice continued to sound in her head. "You can do me a favor and listen to this story."

She did and that night at dinner she told it to Tim and the kids. Becky noticed her younger daughter's eyes shone with pleasure at the descriptions of gunplay. A few days later, the whole family shut down within a few hours of each other, and a few days after that the alien squadron drifted in for a landing at the Home Depot parking lot.

The Bookcase Expedition

I started seeing them during the winter when I was at death's door and wacked out on meds. At first, I thought they were baby praying mantises that had somehow invaded the house to escape the ice and snow, but they were far smaller than that. Minuscule, really. I was surprised I could see them at all. I could, though, and at times with great clarity, as if through invisible binoculars. Occasionally, I heard their distant cries.

I'm talking about fairies, tiny beings in the forms of men, women, and children. I spotted them, thin as a pin and half as tall, creeping about, running from the cats or carrying back to their homes in the walls sacks full of crumbs gathered from our breakfast plates. Mostly I saw them at night, as I had to sit upright in the corner of the living room couch to sleep in order not to suffocate. While the wind howled outside, the light coming in from the kitchen illuminated a small party of them ascending and descending the dunes and craters of the moonscape that was my blanket. One night they planted a flag—a tattered postage stamp fastened to a cat's whisker—into my knee as if I was undiscovered country.

The first time I saw one, it was battling—have you ever seen one of those spiders that looks like it's made of wood? Well, the fairy had a thistle spike and was parrying the picket legs of that arachnid, bravely lunging for its soft underbelly. I took it all in stride, though. I didn't get excited. I certainly didn't go and tell Lynn, who would think it nonsense. "Let the fairies do their thing," I thought. I had way bigger problems to deal with, like trying to breathe.

I know what you're thinking. They weren't a figment of my imagination. For instance, I'd spotted a band of them running along the kitchen counter. They stopped near the edge, where a water glass stood. Together, they pushed against it and toppled it onto the floor. "Ya little bastards," I yelled. They scattered faint atoms of laughter as they fled. The broken glass went everywhere, and I swept for twenty minutes only to find more. The next day, Lynn got a shard in her foot, and I had to burn the end of a needle and operate.

I didn't see them constantly. Sometimes a week would go by before I encountered one. They watched us and I was certain they knew what we were about in our thoughts and acts. I'd spotted them—one with a telescope aimed at my nose and the other sitting, making notes in a bound journal—on the darkened porch floor at night when we sat out wrapped in blankets and candlelight, drinking wine and dozing in the moon glow. I wondered, *Why now, as I trundle toward old age, am I granted the "sight" as my grandma Maisie might have called it?*

A few days ago, I was in my office at the computer trying to iron out my thinking on a story I'd been writing in which there's a scene where a guy, for no reason I could recall, just disappears. There'd been nothing strange about this character previously to give any indication that he was simply going to vanish into thin air. I couldn't remember what I'd had in mind or why at some point it had made sense to me.

The winter illness had stunned my brain. Made me dim and forgetful. Metaphor, simile, were mere words, and I couldn't any longer feel the excitement of their effects. A darkness pervaded my chest and head. I leaned back in my chair away from the computer and turned toward the bookcases. I was concentrating hard not to let the fear of failure in when a damn housefly the size of a grocery-store grape buzzed my left temple, and I slapped myself in the face. It came by again and I ducked, reaching for a magazine with which to do my killing.

That's when a contingent of fairies emerged from the dark half inch of space beneath the middle of the five bookcases that lined the right wall of my office. There was a swarm of them like ants round a drip of ice cream on a summer sidewalk. At first, I thought I wanted to get back to my story, but soon enough I told myself, *You know what? Fuck that story.* I folded my arms and watched. At first they appeared distant, but I didn't fret. I was in no hurry. The clear strong breath of spring had made of the winter a fleeting shadow. I saw out the window—sunlight, blue sky, and a lazy white cloud. The fairies gave three cheers, and I realized something momentous was afoot.

Although I kept my eyes trained on their number, my concentration sharpened and blurred and sharpened again. When my thoughts were away, I have no idea what I was thinking, but when they weren't I was thinking that someday soon I was going to go over to the preserve and walk the two-mile circular path through the golden prairie grass. I decided, in that brief span, it would only be right to take Nellie the dog with me. All this, as I watched the little people, maybe fifty of them, twenty-five on either side, carry out from under a book case the ruler I'd been missing for the past year.

They laid the ruler across a paperback copy of Angela Carter's *Burning Boats.* It had fallen of its own volition from the bottom shelf three days earlier. Sometimes that happens; the books just take a dive. There was a thick anthology of Norse sagas pretty close to it that had been laying there for five months. I made a mental note to, someday soon, rescue the fallen. No time to contemplate it, though, because four fairies broke off from the crowd, climbed atop the Carter collection, and then took a position at the very end of the ruler, facing the bookcase. I leaned forward to get a better look.

The masses moved like water flowing to where the tome of sagas lay. They swept around it, lifting it end over end and standing it upright, upside down, so that the horns of the Viking helmet pictured on the cover pointed to the center of the earth. The next thing I knew, they were toppling the thick book. It came down with the weight of two dozen Norse sagas right onto the end of the ruler opposite from where the fairies stood. Of course, the four of them were shot into the air, arcing toward the bookcase. They flew and each gripped in the right hand a rose-bush thorn.

I watched them hit the wall of books a shelf and a half up and dig the sharp points of their thorns into dust jackets and spines. One of them made a tear in the red cover of my hard-back copy of *Black Hole.* Once secured, I noticed them hitch themselves at the waist with a rope belt to their affixed thorn. I'd not noticed before, but they had bows and arrows, and spools of thread from Lynn's sewing basket draped across their chests like bandoliers. I had a sudden memory of the Teeny Weenies, a race of fairies that appeared in the *Daily News* Sunday Comics when I was a kid. I envisioned for a moment an old panel from the *Weenies* in which one was riding a wild turkey with a saddle and reins while the others gathered giant acorns half their size. I came back from that thought just in time to see all four fairies release their arrows into the ceiling of the shelf they were on. I heard the distant, petite impact of each shaft. Then, bows slung over their shoulders, they began to climb, hand over hand, using the book spines in front of them to rappel upward.

Since their purpose seemed to be to ascend, I foresaw trouble ahead for them. The next shelf above, which they'd have to somehow flip up onto, held two rows of books, not one, so there was no clear space for them to land. They'd have to flip up and again dig in with their thorns and attach themselves to the spines of books whose bottoms stuck perilously out over the edge of the shelf. When I considered the agility and strength all this took, I shook my head and put my hand over my heart. I wanted to see them succeed, though, and went off on a trail of musing that pitted the reliability of the impossible against the potential chaos of reality. A point came where I wandered from the path of my thoughts and wound up witnessing the smallest of the fairies nearly plummet to his death. I felt his scream in my liver.

The poor little fellow had lost a hold on his thread line and was hanging out over the abyss, desperately grasping a poorly planted thorn in the spine of *Blind Man with a Pistol.* His compatriot, whom I just then realized was a woman with long dark hair, shot an arrow into the ceiling of the shelf. Once she had that line affixed to her belt, she swung over to her comrade in danger and put her left arm around him. He let go his thorn spike and swung with her. I was so intent upon watching this rescue that I missed but from the very corner of my eye one of the other tiny adventurers fall. His (for I was just then somehow certain it was a he, and his name was Meeshin) minuscule weight dragged the book he'd attached to off the shelf after him. This was the thing about the fairies; if you could see them, the longer you looked, the deeper you knew them: their names, their motivations, their secrets.

I only turned in time to see that he'd been crushed by the slim volume of *Quiet Days in Clichy.* I watched to see if his compatriots from beneath the bookshelf would appear to claim his corpse, but they didn't. The loneliness of Meeshin's death affected me more than it should have. It came to me that he was married and had three fairy kids. His art was whittling totem poles full of animals of the imagination out of toothpicks. I'd wondered where all my toothpicks had gone. I pictured his wife, Tibith, in the fairy marketplace telling a friend that all Meeshin's crazy creatures could be seen, like in a gallery, way in the back of the cupboard beneath the kitchen sink. Last I saw him behind my eyes, it was night and he lay quietly in bed, his arms around his wife.

Next I caught up with the climbers, the three had gathered to rest on the top edge of a book back in the second row of that dangerous shelf. I shifted my position in the chair and craned my neck a bit to see that the volume in question was Paulo Coelho's *The Alchemist,* a book I'd never read and one of those strange additions to my library, the acquisition of which, was a mystery. My favorite essayist, Alberto Manguel, had said that he'd never enter a library that contained a book by Coelho. I thought that on the off chance he might travel to the drop edge of yonder, Ohio, I should get rid of it.

I knew them all by name now and something about their little lives. The woman with the long dark hair, Aspethia, was the leader of the expedition. I wasn't sure what the purpose of their journey was, but I knew it had a purpose. It was a mission given to her directly by Magorian, the Fairy Queen. Her remaining companions were the little fellow she rescued, Sopso, and a large fellow, Balthazar, who wore a conical hat with a chin strap like something from a child's birthday party on his bald head. Aspethia spoke words of encouragement to Sopso, who cowered on his knees for fear of falling. She went into her pack and pulled out another rose thorn for him. "Now, if we don't hurry, there will be no point in our having come this far," she said.

The next shelf up they found easy purchase at the front as there was only one row of books pushed all the way back. It was the shelf with my collection of the Lang fairy books, each volume a different color. That they all stood together was the only bit of authentic order in my library. I watched the fairies pass in front of the various colors—red, violet, green, orange—and wondered if they knew the books were more than merely giant rocks to be climbed. Did they know these boulders they passed held the ancient stories of their species? I pictured the huge boulder, like the egg of a roc, sitting alone amidst the golden grass over at the preserve and daydreamed about the story it might hatch.

The afternoon pushed on with the slow, steady progress of a fairy climbing thread. They moved up the various shelves of the bookcase, one after the other, with a methodical pace. Even the near falls, the brushes with death, were smooth and timely.

There were obstacles, books I'd placed haphazardly atop a row pretending that I intended to someday reshelve them. When the companions were forced to cross my devil tambourine, which had sat there on the fifth level since two Halloweens previously, it made their teensy steps echo in the caverns of the shelves. The big one, Balthazar, skewered, with a broken broom straw, a silverfish atop one of the Smiley novels, and they lit a fairy fire, which only cooked their meal but didn't burn, thank God. Those three remaining climbers sat in a circle and ate the cooked insect. While they did, Sopso read from a book so infinitesimally small it barely existed.

I closed my eyes and drifted off into the quiet of the afternoon. The window was open a bit and a breeze snaked in around me. Moments later, I bolted awake, and the first thing I did was search the bookshelf for the expedition. When I found them, a pulse of alarm shot up my back. Balthazar and Aspethia were battling an oni netsuke come miraculously to life. I'd had the thing for years. Lynn bought it for me in a store in Chinatown in Philly across the street from Joe's Peking Duck House. It was a cheap imitation, made to look like ivory from some kind of resin—a short, stocky demon with a dirty face and horns. He held a mask of his own visage in his right hand and a big bag in his left. He tried to scoop the fairies into it. Sopso was nowhere in sight.

Seeing an inanimate object come to life made me a little dizzy, and I think I was trembling. The demon growled and spat at them. What was more incredible still was the fact that the companions were able to drive the monster to the edge of the shelf. The fighting was fierce, the fairies drawing blood with long daggers fashioned from the ends of brass safety pins. The demon's size gave it the advantage, and more than once he'd scooped Balthazar and Aspethia up but they'd managed to wriggle out of the eyeholes of the mask before he could bag them. The little people sang a lilting fairy anthem throughout the battle that I only caught garbled snatches of. They ran as they sang in circles round the giant, poking him in the hairy shins and toes and Achilles tendon with their daggers.

Oni lost his balance and tipped a jot toward the edge. In a blink, Balthaszar leaped up, put a foot on the demon's belly, grabbed its beard in his free hand, pulled himself higher, and plunged the dagger into his enemy's eye. The demon reeled backward, screaming, turning in circles. Aspethia leaped forward and drove her dagger to the hilt in Oni's left testicle. That elicited a terrible cry, and then the creature tipped over the edge of the shelf. Balthazar tried to leap off to where Aspethia stood, but Oni grabbed his leg and they went all the way down together. Although the fairy's neck was broken, his party hat remained undamaged.

Aspethia crawled to the edge of the shelf and peered down the great distance to see the fate of her comrade. If she survived the expedition, she would be the one responsible for telling Balthazar's wife and children of his death. She sat back away from the edge and took a deep breath. Sopso emerged from a cavern between *The Book of Contemplation* and Harry Crews's *Childhood.* He walked over to where Aspethia knelt and put his hand on her shoulder. She reached up and grabbed it. He helped her to her feet and they made their way uneventfully to the top shelf. As they climbed, I looked back down at the fallen netsuke and saw that it had regained its original form of a lifeless figurine. Had there been a demon in it? How and why did it come to life? The gift of seeing fairies comes wrapped in questions.

On the top shelf, they headed north toward the back wall of the room, passing a foot-high Ghost Rider plastic figure, the marble Ganesh bookends, a small picture frame containing a block of Jason Van Hollander's Hell Stamps, Flannery O'Connor's letters, and *Our Lady of the Flowers* shelved without consciousness of design on my part directly next to *Our Lady of Darkness.* A copy of the writings of Cotton Mather lay atop the books of that shelf, its upper half forming an overhang beneath which the expedition had to pass. Its cover held a portrait of Mather from his own time and faced down. Eyes peered from above. His brows, his nose, his powdered wig, but not his mouth, bore witness to the fairies passing. For a moment, I was with them in the shadow, staring up at the preacher's gaze, incredulous as to how the glance of the image was capable of following us.

Eventually, they came to where the last bookcase in the row butts up against the northern wall. Aspethia and Sopso stroked the barrier as if it had some religious significance. She leaned over and put her arm around Sopso's shoulder, turned him, and pointed out the framed painting hanging on the northern wall about two feet from the bookcase. He saw it and nodded. The painting in question had been given to me by my friend Barney, who painted it in his studio at Dividing Creek in South Jersey. It's a knock-off of a Charles Willson Peale painting of the artist ascending a staircase, only Barney's is done in green, and there's only one figure—a ghost with the acrimonious face of John Ashcroft, President Bush's secretary of state, looking back over his shoulder.

She shot an arrow into the northern wall just above the middle of where the painting hung. She leaned forward and Sopso climbed upon her back. With the line from the arrow tight in her hands, she inched toward the edge of the bookcase. She jumped and they swung toward the painting, Sopso screaming, and crashed into the image where Ashcroft's ascot met his second chin. Once they'd stopped bouncing against the canvas, she told her passenger to tighten his grip. He did and she began hauling both of them to the top of the picture frame. Her climbing looked like magic.

For some reason, right here, I recalled the strange sound I'd heard behind the garage the last few nights. A wheezing growl that reverberated through the night. I pictured the devil crouching back there in the shadows, but our neighbor told us it was a fox in heat. It sounded like a cry from another world. My interest in it faded, and in a heartbeat my focus was back on the painting. They had achieved the top of the frame and were resting. I wondered where the expedition was headed next. There was another painting on that wall about four feet away from the ghost on the staircase. It was a painting of Garuda by my younger son. The distance between the paintings was vast in fairy feet. I couldn't believe they would attempt to cross to it. Aspethia showed it no interest, but instead pointed straight up.

She took her bow, knocked an arrow with a thread line in place, and aimed it at the ceiling. My glance followed the path of the potential shot, and only then did I notice that her arrow was aimed precisely into a prodigious spider web that stretched from directly above the painting all the way to the corner of the north wall. She released the arrow, and I tried to follow it but caught only a blur. It hit its mark, and that drew my attention to the fact that right next to where it hit, that fly, big as a grape, was trapped in webbing and buzzing to beat the band. I looked along the web to the corner of the ceiling and saw the spider, skinny legs with a fat white pearl of an abdomen. I could see it drooling as it moved forward to finally claim its catch.

It surprised me when, without hesitation, Sopso alone climbed the line toward the ceiling. He shimmied up at a pace that lapped the spider's progress, the rose thorn clenched in his teeth. The fly was well-wrapped in spider silk, unable to use its wings, its cries muffled. The pale spider danced along the vibrating strands. Sopso reached the fly and cut away enough web to get his legs around the insect's back. Too bad he was upside down. The spider advanced while the fairy continued to hack away. I was able to hear every strand he cut—the noise of a spring spung, like an effect from a cartoon. The way Sopso worked, with such courage and cool, completely reversed my estimation of him. Till then, I'd thought of him as a burden to the expedition, but, after all, he had his place.

I was at the edge of my seat, my neck craned and my head tilted back. My heart was pounding. The spider reared back, poised to strike, and Sopso never flinched but worked methodically in the looming shadow of death. Fangs shut and four piercing sharp leg points struck at nothing. The fairy had cut the last strand and he, legs around the back of the fly, fell upside down toward the floor. At the last second the fly's wings worked, and they managed to pull out of the death plunge. They shot up past my left ear toward the ceiling. Aspethia, the spider, and I followed their erratic course. They zigzagged with great buzzing all around the room, but when they passed over the bookcase near the window of the west wall, the fairy, afraid the dizzy fly would crash, jumped off and landed safely on a copy of Albahari's *Leeches.*

Sopso was stranded. He and Aspethia waved to each other across the incredible expanse of my office. They might as well have been on different worlds. Each cried out but neither was able to hear the other. Her arrows could not reach him. He had with him no thread bandoliers, nor even a pin-tip knife. Without them, there was no way he could climb down from that height, and by the time Aspethia returned to the fairy village and could mount a rescue party, he would most likely die of starvation. Still, she set out quickly to get back home on the slim chance he might survive long enough. He watched her go, and I could see the sadness come over him. The sight of it left me with a terrible chill.

What was I to do? My heart went out to the lost climber who gave his life to save an insignificant fly, not to mention brave Aspethia. I thought how easily I could change everything for them. I stood up and stepped over to the bookcase by the window on the west wall. I reached out to gently lift Sopso in order to place him down on the floor across the room near where the expedition had begun. My fingers closed, and for no good reason, he suddenly disappeared. A moment of silence passed, and then I heard a chorus well up from beneath the bookcases, each voice not but a pinprick of laughter.

Later that evening, as Lynn and I sat on the porch in the last pink glow of sunset, she reached across the glass-topped table that held our wine and said, “Look here.” She was holding something between her thumb and forefinger. Whatever she was showing me was very delicate and what with the failing light I needed to lean in close to see. To my shock it was a cat whisker with a postage stamp affixed to the end, like a tiny flag.

Her expression made me ask, “How long have you known?”

She laughed quietly. “Way back,” she said and her words cut away the webbing that had trapped me.

The Winter Wraith

(for Kit Reed)

Henry sensed resignation in the posture of the Christmas tree. It slouched toward the living-room window as if peering out. There was no way he could plug its lights in, cheer it up. The thing was dryer than the Sandman's mustache, its spine a stick of kindling. The least vibration brought a shower of needles. Ornaments fell of their own accord. Some broke, which he had to sweep and vacuum, initiating the descent of more needles, more ornaments. The cat took some as toys and batted them around the kitchen floor. Glittering evidence in the field indicated Bothwell, the dog, had acquired a taste for tinsel.

Mero had told him not to take it down. She had a special way she wrapped the ornaments when boxing them and he wasn't about to argue for doing it by himself. At the end of that first week she was away in China, though, the presence of the tree became an imposition. He described it in his Friday journal as, "A distant cousin, once accused of pyromania, arriving for an indefinite visit."

In the middle of his work, in the middle of the grocery store, when walking around the lake with the dog, the spirit of that sagging pine was always waiting by the front window in the living room of his thoughts. Then Mero finally called on FaceTime from Shanghai. Her image was distorted, as if he were seeing her through rippling water. In a heartbeat, the picture froze, but she kept talking. He told her he missed her and she said the same. She said Shanghai was amazing, enormous, and that she liked the young woman who was her translator and guide. She asked about Bothwell. Henry spoke about the freezing wind, the snow. She told him to be careful driving, and then he told her about the tree. "It's shot," he said. "I gotta take it down."

Suddenly the call cut out and he couldn't get her back. He wanted to tell her he loved her and hear her voice some more, but in a way he understood. It was like dialing another world. The distance between Ohio and Shanghai made him shiver.

He called Bothwell, and the border collie appeared. "Do you want to go for a walk?" he asked. The dog's blue eyes were intense and it cocked its head to the side as if to say, "What do you think?" So Henry put his coat and hat and mittens on, and out they went, over the snow, across the yard, through the orchard, past the garden, into the farmer's winter fields that surrounded the property. Corn stubble and snow stretched out to the horizon in three directions. It was sundown, orange and pink in the west, a deep royal blue to the east where he spotted the moon.

They headed toward the windbreak of white oak about a quarter mile into the field. The frozen gusts that blew across the open land sliced right through him, and he struggled to hold closed his jacket with the broken zipper. They entered the thicket of giant old trees. Under the clacking, empty branches, last light turned to mist and shadow. He sat down on a fallen log and looked to the west. Bothwell sniffed around and then sat behind him to escape the gusts that eddied among the trees. Henry had a hell of a time lighting a cigarette. Once he got it going, though, he made an executive decision. The first part was to open a bottle of wine when he got back to the house, the second to dismantle the tree and get rid of it by the following afternoon.

He pictured how he would do it. Put the ornaments in a pile on the dining-room table. Cover them with a tablecloth to hide them from the cat and leave them there till Mero got back. Pull the lights free. Grab off the cursed tinsel in handfuls. Kick the tree in the spleen and wrestle it to the floor. Remove the base. Drag the corpse through the dining room, the kitchen, to the sliding door. Deposit the remains out back in the snow. Burn incense to mask the odor of rotted Christmas. Sweep and vacuum. Two hours for the whole ordeal, he figured, and spoke into the wind, "Adios, motherfucker."

Then Bothwell made a strange noise and Henry felt something behind him. He stood up quickly and turned, glimpsing what looked in the dimmest of light like a wolf. Gray and tan, bushy coat. It skulked around a tree and disappeared. He knew there were no wolves in Ohio, but the creature was too big for a coyote. The idea of it sneaking about in the dark sent a shot of adrenaline through him and his heart pounded. He called to the dog and they left the trees in a rush. Somewhere between the smoke and the wolf, night had dropped. Unable to see where he was stepping, he twisted his leg on corn stubble and his knee began to ache. He hobbled toward the light of the house, peering over his shoulder every few yards. By the time he reached the kitchen he could hardly walk. He pulled the cork on a bottle of Malbec standing on one leg.

Grabbing a glass and the bottle, he hopped into the living room. The tree was waiting for him. As he sat on the couch, a shower of needles fell, followed by an ornament. It hit a branch on the way down, shattering into three jagged scoops and a handful of glitter. He watched it happen, knew it was the ornament Mero had bought for their first Christmas together. He decided in an instant that he'd wait till spring to tell her. Bothwell came in and curled up by his feet. Henry drank wine and turned on the TV.

He woke suddenly hours later to the dark, in bed. His mouth was dry. He had no recollection of getting off the couch and coming upstairs. Looking at the clock, he saw it was only 3:13. He laid his head back on the pillow and closed his eyes. That's when he realized there was a quiet but distinct rhythmic noise coming from downstairs. He could barely hear it, like a voice whispering a touch too loud. The first thing he did was call to

Bothwell for courage. The dog was already at his side of the bed. Henry sat up, put his feet on the floor, and listened. The voice continued mumbling on and then broke out into a cry for help: one long, extended scream diminishing into silence, followed by a loud thud.

Henry jumped up, his heart racing, his hair—what there was of it—tingling. He reached for the wooden baton he kept behind the night table next to the bed. At the top of the stairs, he stood aside and let the dog go first. He took each step slowly, protecting his bad knee and in no hurry to find out what was going on. Before he reached the bottom, it struck him that the noise must have been coming from the TV he'd never turned off. This made him brave, and, holding his weapon in front of him, he limped boldly into the living room.

The light was still on. "Great," he said, gazing down upon the fallen Christmas tree. Although it had slouched so long toward the window, when it fell, it went over backwards, across the middle of the living-room floor. Ornaments everywhere. The useless water in the metal base had soaked into the carpet. The dry needle fallout was epic. He looked at the dog. The dog looked at him. Henry stepped forward and kicked the tree. It shuddered, dropping more of itself. He shook his head and looked across the room. The TV was off.

He and Bothwell searched each of the downstairs rooms, just to be on the safe side, then Henry started a pot of coffee. He decided not to wait for morning but to dive in right now, dismantle the thing, and get it out of the house. While the coffee brewed, he cleared the dining-room table and took another look at the remains. Leaning against the archway connecting living room and dining room, he told himself he'd just have to get his head around it. He went and poured himself a cup of coffee and came back to sit on the couch. The cat, Turtle, was at the other end. It struck Henry that she'd probably sat through the entire misadventure—the tree weaving, gasping, calling out for help, and then crashing to the floor. He remembered her sitting in the same position when he'd lumbered down the stairs. "Please don't get too worked up over anything," he said to the cat. Turtle looked at him and then stood. At that moment, the TV came on. Henry lurched and grunted in surprise. The cat jumped down from the couch, and he saw that she had been lying on the remote.

His hands found the needles sharper than when the tree was alive. He fetched the rubber gloves from beneath the kitchen sink and put them on. The work proved exhausting, all that bending and the often tedious exercise of untwining an ornament hanger from a branch. At times he had to wrestle the dead weight of the thing, rolling it to retrieve ornaments crushed beneath it, lifting it to open the sharp branches so he could reach in and rescue the angel from where she'd fallen into the belly of the beast. Don't forget the icicles, he heard Mero say in his mind. Plastic icicles, thin as pipe cleaners, perfectly transparent. There were six. After locating four, he said "Fuck it" and gave up.

At sunrise of a bitter, overcast day, Henry dragged the tree through the dining room and kitchen, then out the sliding door. Despite the fiercely howling wind, in his haste to finish the job he left his jacket inside and was dressed only in a T-shirt. As he slid the corpse over the fresh fall of snow, it left a wake of brown needles. Depositing it next to the garden shed, he took a few steps back. He'd made sure earlier to slip on his boots, so he charged forward and kicked the tree. His boot slid under the trunk and lifted it into the air. His next move would have been a crushing stomp to the midsection, but when he brought his foot down, the bad knee of his other leg went out, and he slipped on the snow and fell.

After sweeping and vacuuming and moving the coffee table and chairs back in front of the window, he lay down on the couch and grabbed the remote. Not even 10:00 a.m. and he found Jack Palance in black and white, *The House of Numbers*. He maneuvered the couch pillow under his head, then closed his eyes and let the sound of the twins-and-prison plot lead him to sleep. He woke at 4:15 p.m. and glanced at the window. From his supine position, all he could see was the dark gray sky. He heard the wind, though, and before he got up and looked, he knew it was snowing, big flakes angling down from the west.

He went to the kitchen and made a fresh pot of coffee. Still dazed from sleep, he leaned against the kitchen sink and stared out the window. He watched the empty branches bend, and in the distance, across the field, the world filled up with snow. "The new ice age," he said to his reflection. When his gaze shifted to the garden shed, he blinked and looked again. He leaned over forward to get his glasses closer to the glass. For a moment, he went so numb that even his knee stopped aching.

This time he put on his jacket and hat and mittens. He called for Bothwell and together they went out the sliding door. The snow was on its way to becoming ice and the wind was fierce. Covering his face with one arm, he made his way toward the garden shed. He believed the tree was still there, just covered by a small drift. When he reached the spot where he'd dumped it, he turned his back to the wind and looked down. Seeing a rise in the snow, he toed the white mound but felt nothing beneath it. A minute later, he'd cleared the spot, pushing the snow aside with his boots, and was staring at frozen ground.

"Where?" he said to Bothwell, and although he laughed, a current of fear cut through the confusion. He looked up quickly and scanned the darkening yard to see if the thing had been blown away. The wind on the plains was strong enough—over the summer it had lifted a table on the patio and flipped it, turning its glass top into jagged, ice-like chips. Seeing no sign of the corpse in the distance, he started back into the orchard to check the shadows beneath the trees. He and Bothwell walked around the entire property but found nothing, save that at some point he'd left the garage light on.

Entering the garage through the side door, he found instant relief from the snow and wind. Bothwell followed him in. Henry looked over the stacks of unopened boxes he'd never unpacked after moving in two years earlier. It was all books, thousands of them. He smelled their damp molder and had a memory flash of the warehouse scene at the end of *Citizen Kane.* A scrabbling sound followed fast by a desperate squeal came from far back in the hangar-sized structure. The dog barked. Henry flipped the light off and they headed into the house.

Later, sitting in his office in front of his computer and sipping coffee, he leaned back and took a break from the irritation of his writing. His thoughts wandered and he pictured the Christmas tree miles away in the dark, slouching through drifts to the edge of Route 70 and sticking out a branch. "Cali or the North Pole?" Henry considered the desiccated pine's journey west—the truckers, the rest stops, the mountain vistas—until his reverie was interrupted by a horrendous clank that shuddered through the house from somewhere below. Bothwell leaped up from where he was lying near the door, his ears at attention.

Henry wished he'd brought the baton upstairs. Still, the noise didn't sound like someone forcing a door or window. It had that unmistakable sense of finality to it, as if the God of Trouble had smote some major appliance once and for all. *Burst pipe? Water heater? Something electric?* He ran through a list as he limped downstairs, Bothwell leading the way. The lights in the hallway, living room, dining room, kitchen all came on when he flipped their switches, and he was grateful for that. He looked around to see if Turtle had knocked over a vase or picture frame, maybe slid a glass off the counter in the bathroom, but for once the cat was innocent. The front-porch door and sliding door in the back were both locked. He ran the water to check for a lack of pressure but the flow was steady and strong.

The dog followed him around the kitchen as he searched for the flashlight. "This is unparalleled bullshit," he said to Bothwell, who could barely hide his excitement over the promise of action at such a late hour. It took Henry twenty minutes to go through the various kitchen-junk drawers, checking each at least twice before he found the flashlight. Another ten minutes went on locating batteries. The beam it emitted when finally operational was a vague pretense of light. He found the baton where he'd left it in the living room and then went into the hallway, to the basement door. He opened it. "Forsake all hope," he said to the dog.

Standing at the top of those worn steps leading into darkness, an image of the tree returned to him, and this time it wasn't headed west. This time, it had never left. A reek of dampness and subtle mildew rolled up and engulfed him. He thought of the horror movie basement cliché as he flipped on the light switch and took his first step. Turtle appeared out of nowhere and brushed past him, a black blur diving down the stairs. "No!" he yelled after the cat, but that was pointless.

The house was over a hundred years old and he'd never heard of a "wet basement" before they bought it. Back in Jersey, where they'd come from, the words "wet basement" would have been a deal-breaker. But old farmhouses weren't built with rec rooms or indoor Ping-Pong tables in mind. The basement was basically a foundational necessity, a place to store things raised up on pallets, since water was expected at certain times of the year. Henry had to duck as he stepped beneath the lintel. There was one dim lightbulb hanging from a chain in the middle of the main part of a concrete chamber.

He used the baton to rip down a prodigious cobweb as he made his way from one appliance to the next, laying his hand lightly on each to see if it was trembling with life. The water heater was fine and the dehumidifier was doing its thing. Then he touched the furnace. It was silent, no vibration, stone cold. "That ain't good," he said. The dog sat down on the bottom step, as if reluctant to commit a paw to the underground. Henry flipped on the flashlight and moved toward the dark recesses of the cellar and the adjoining concrete closet without a door, a narrow space where the fuse box hung.

Often, during spring, the water rose in that niche as high as four or five inches, and he'd once seen a toad hop out of it into the greater basement. Luckily the ground outside was frozen and the floor dry. He ran the beam of the flashlight over the different fuses to see if one had popped, but they were all unmarked and he really had no idea what he was looking for. Mero was the one who always dealt with the fuses.

"We're gonna freeze our asses off tonight," he said. When he stepped back into the basement, he noticed Bothwell retreating up the stairs. "Traitor," he shouted, intending to follow as quickly as possible. As he headed toward the steps, however, he realized he had no idea where Turtle had gotten to. He aimed the tepid beam into dark corners and made the psss-psss-psss noise Mero always used to summon the cat. After two dozen pssses, he called out, "You can stay down here all winter, then." As he made for the steps, he heard a meow. He turned and aimed the beam at a spot on the wall next to the water heater.

He'd forgotten the hole there, a roughly foot-and-a-half-by-one-foot gap in the concrete that led into the foundation. Why it was there, he had no idea. He wondered if perhaps a pipe had been shoved through from outside at some point. Or a poorly covered-over coal chute, maybe? He stepped up to it and shone the light inside. Turtle's green eyes caught the weak glow and made the most of it. She was about four feet into the tunnel. He tried another "Psss-psss-psss." A meow answered. "Come on, Turtle," he said. "Come on." Every time he made the psss noise, the cat meowed but stayed where it was. "I hate you," he told her. The bright green eyes blinked.

When the cat finally moved, she did so slowly. She appeared at the opening and leaped down onto the floor. That's when he distinctly heard the porch door open with a bang, heard the whoosh of the storm enter the kitchen above. He was sure of it. He felt the burst of adrenaline shoot through him, yet he was stiff with fear. There was no spit to swallow. The harder he gripped the baton, the less he believed he would be able to wield it if he had to. Bothwell backed down the stairs into view. His hackles were up and he was growling. Henry heard footsteps and dropped the flashlight. He managed to creep to the bottom of the steps. "If you leave now, I won't shoot you," he shouted. "The police are on their way."

There was more movement above but he couldn't track it. Just one slow, clomping footstep after another. Out of some perverse impulse, he made his move. Gripping the baton, he raised it over his head and lurched up the stairs in a woefully executed surprise attack. Using his elbows on the door jambs, he propelled himself in a stumble down the hall and into the kitchen, Bothwell barking at his side. "Swing for the fence," Henry whispered.

The door was wide open and the cold air swept in around him. He went to it immediately and shut it. Only one step ahead of paralyzing fear, he knew he couldn't rest, plunging into room after room, expecting the intruder in every one. In the downstairs bedroom, he instructed Bothwell to look under the bed. They checked all the closets. When Turtle jumped out from behind the shower curtain, Henry flailed with the baton and destroyed a towel rack.

Upstairs, out of breath, his knee screaming, he made the rounds of all the rooms but found no one. Half relieved, he said "What a night" to the dog as they made their way down from the second floor. Back in the kitchen, he looked for his phone and found it on the counter. Without relinquishing the baton, he dialed the police. There was a long span of silence and then the line sparked with static. He tried to get through twice more and gave up. "Here's another forklift full of shit," he told Bothwell, tossing the phone on the counter. The dog's expression as much as said, "You're getting a little dramatic now." Henry nodded in agreement and paused to think it through. That's when he noticed something he'd missed earlier: the kitchen floor was littered with brown needles. He'd been so intent on attack, he'd trodden right through them, never looking down.

He gripped the baton, and Bothwell tensed. The trail of brown needles led off into the dining room. Man and dog moved slowly, quietly toward the darkened entrance. He could have sworn he'd left all the lights on downstairs. He stopped and listened. No sound except the wind. Lifting the baton, he flipped the light switch. Instinctively crouching, he tensed against an assault—if only from the sudden light. When Bothwell didn't bark, Henry knew there was no one there. The house was perfectly still.

"Nothing," he said to the dog, and decided to make yet another pot of coffee. Before he could move, though, some speck of brightness caught his eye and drew his gaze to the dining-room table. The dark green cloth resembled a miniature landscape, what with the ornaments trapped beneath it. He stepped closer. There were brown needles scattered amid the rolling hills, and in one of the more prominent valleys lay, side by side, the two missing icicles he'd abandoned on the tree. He reached out but didn't touch them.

"Come on, now," he said to the ceiling.

He muttered through two glasses of wine, his breath becoming vapor in the especially frigid air of the kitchen, and the cold finally drove him to forsake the bottle. He wrapped up in three blankets and propped himself in a corner of the couch with the lights out. The baton lay only inches away on the coffee table. Bothwell was next to him, curled in a ball, and Turtle stretched out along the rim of the pillow on which he rested his head. After a while, his eyes adjusted and he could see the snow coming down again beyond the window. At some point he heard the heater kick back on and the dog gave a whimper of appreciation. When he shut his eyes to better hear the voices in the wind, sleep took him like an avalanche, and he wound up in the back seat of a cab, streaking along the main street of Shanghai, on his way to meet Mero for lunch.

Big Dark Hole

The school and its fields that are the basic setting of this story don't exist anymore. They were turned into a housing development about forty years ago. I suppose most of the teachers, if not all, are dead. The principal, Mr. Torey, who had a habit of rubbing his throat like the ghost of a hanged man, collapsed in the *15 Items or Less* aisle at the King Kullen grocery store five years after I graduated high school. A guy who'd been in the math class I'd failed twice and he failed along with me (I forget his last name but his first name was Jeeb) told me about Torey's demise at a party one night while we were sharing a joint in the basement of this girl's house. He told me Torey suddenly leaned against the checkout counter like he'd been punched in the gut and on his way to the floor croaked, "Why?"

Sewer Pipe Hill lay at the edge of the woods, a pregnancy of naked dirt that rose out of the ground and was a perfect launching spot to test out racers. We made go-carts with bicycle training wheels, old baby carriage wheels, the wheels from shopping carts, and wooden milk cartons with one side banged out for a seat, rope for steering, and two-by-fours rescued from the demolition of the dead witch's shack deep in the woods where the sassafras grew. When we took the boards from her partially dismantled home, we set what was left standing on fire and ran like only we could through the trails and over the fallen trees, through the sticker-bush tunnels.

The witch was in my dreams after that for a while. She really did look like a witch—pimply face and a long nose. She yelled at us in a foreign language and came out of her place with her cane and kerchief and long coat to chase us. When we were just about out from under the trees and sprinting across the school fields, I always heard her laugh, an urgent bird call, an icy hand on the back of my neck. How long had she lived there? A long, long time.

The racers we made weren't too fast and they invariably crashed at the bottom of the south slope of the hill where it dipped into a three-foot straight drop. It wasn't about who had the best time but who had the most glorious crash. My brother was in the lead because he was the most dramatic. Whereas Bill Gorman and Lorel Manzo survived worse hits and wipeouts, my brother screamed, flailed his arms as he fell, and followed it up with copious moaning. We were all doubled over, laughing at him. The other kids were even willing to hand him the victory. We ran down the hill to help him out of the wreck of our racer.

That's when Regina Manzo called out, "Hey, David, what are you doing?" There was David Gorman, bare chested, sneakers and socks already off, removing his khaki shorts. He stood before the maw of the sewer pipe, staring into that big, dark, hole. His brother yelled at him to put his pants on. The older Manzo girl, Lorel, covered her eyes and turned away, but Regina stared and smiled. David walked up to the sewer pipe, knelt into it on all fours, and robotically proceeded to crawl forward into the darkness.

"Come back or I'm telling Mom," his brother called after him. By the time we made it to the opening of the pipe, all we caught was a flash of his white underwear before he disappeared into the black. "Come back," we called. "Come back." "There's spiders in there."

"I like spiders," his voice came quietly echoing to us.

"I'm gonna call the cops," yelled Lorel.

"What a knucklehead," my brother said to Bill Gorman.

Bill was in a panic. His parents left him in charge of David all day and were pretty unforgiving if things went wrong. Tears ran down his face. He screamed, "Shut up or I'll beat you."

Regina Manzo said, "We can catch him up at the manhole cover." She took off running up the hill to the field and followed the asphalt walkway that led toward the school's playground. We tried to catch her, but she was the fastest girl on record. When she reached the spot in the walkway where the round, rusted cover was, she dropped to her knees, leaned forward to put her mouth close to the small hole cut at the rim of it, and shouted. I think she called out his name. When we showed up, she'd turned her head and put her ear to the hole.

"What'd he say?" asked Bill.

"He said to leave him alone," said Regina.

Bill told Lorel to get on her bike and go tell her mom to call the cops.

"Don't tell me what to do," said Lorel. "You're not my husband."

"Quick," Bill cried, "before somebody flushes and he's drowned."

My brother took off back toward the hill to fetch his bike.

Bill shoved Regina out of the way and yelled down into the pipe," What are you doing?"

David must have been right beneath us then. I heard his reply squeeze through the small opening in the manhole cover. His voice rang like an echo in a tin cavern. He said, "Figuring."

Regina, me, and Lorel all laughed. Even Bill laughed for a second, and then he threatened us that we better shut up.

We stood there in the autumn breeze and sharp sunlight beneath a blue sky in silence until a little while went by and the police showed up. They came in the eastern side entrance to the school fields, having traveled down the packed dirt trail that was Cowpath Road, an ancient route through the woods. They rolled over the remains of broken bottles recently shattered by Bobby Lerner and his gang. Everyone but the adults knew Bobby had a gun and a pocket full of bullets and him and Bobby Shaw and Cho-cho and Mike Wolfe took target practice on forty-ounce

Colt 45 bottles they'd emptied. My brother told me just that week he was surprised no one had been shot yet because, as he said, "Lerner's a totally crazy motherfucker."

The cops came on, and I was hoping they'd flash the lights, but they didn't. As they inched across the field (good thing nobody was dying), Regina ran toward them waving her arms over her head, her braids bouncing. When she reached them, they stopped and told her to get in the back seat, and she did.

There were two cops. We all knew them. They were often at the school to give talks about not getting into cars with strange people or not smoking cigarettes. The big one with the dough face, Officer Flapp, seemed stupid as the day is long, even to me at ten years old. The other was taller, thinner, with a kind of rodent face. His upper teeth hung over his bottom lip and he wore murky glasses. They weren't sunglasses, you know, with lenses that look black in the sun. They were sort of light brown. You could still see through them to where his beady, weasel eyes rapidly shifted back and forth. We called him Officer Weezer, because he looked like a weasel. He spoke first as they got out of the car. Flapp opened and held the door for Regina.

"What have we got here?" His eyes were going a mile a minute behind his shitty glasses.

"David Gorman's in the sewer pipes," blurted Lorel Manzo.

"He's down there?" said the Weeze, pointing at the ground.

"He's moved on," said Regina. "He was here a few minutes ago. Who knows where he is now."

"You gotta find him, please," said Bill to the cops.

Weeze told Flapp, "Call the fire department."

"Aye, aye," was the response, a lot slower than it's supposed to be.

"Why's he doing this?" asked Weeze.

"He's figuring," said Regina and laughed.

"Jesus," said the cop and shook his head. "Flapp, tell them to bring Porkchops," he called to his partner.

A few minutes later the firetruck pulled through the front gates of the school and up over the curb with my brother following on his bike. The siren whooped twice as they approached. I thought they were gonna bring lunch from what Officer Weezer had said, but Porkchops turned out to be this stout, fat hound, like a black and white beer keg on legs. The driver of the firetruck didn't get out of the cab but rolled down the window and lit up a cigarette. Two other firemen climbed off the back of the truck, all done up—boots, helmets, yellow jackets. Flapp and the Weeze told the firemen what was going on while we listened in. Then Weeze led the way toward Sewer Pipe Hill, Regina Manzo running out in front of them, skipping, doing cartwheels.

It was afternoon by then and the sun was warm even though it was early October. We gathered at the big dark hole and gazed in. Without anything being said, Porkchops walked up to the concrete face the sewer pipe was set in and pissed on it. Then he crawled up into the hole and proceeded forward at the same rate as David Gorman.

"Does that dog know what it's doing?" asked Officer Weezer.

The fireman with the big mustache shrugged.

A minute later, we heard Porkchops barking in the distance beneath the ground.

"If someone flushes, will he drown?" Bill asked, tears in his eyes again.

The cops and firemen cracked up. Officer Flapp said, "Your mother should've flushed."

Come that evening, they weren't laughing anymore. Me and my brother eventually went home for dinner, and when we returned to the field there were three cop cars, two more firetrucks and an ambulance. The local tv reporters were there, Mr. Torey was there, and most of our neighbors who lived by the school. At one point they had a dozen men crawling through the sewer pipes, cops, firemen, special rescue workers.

Mr. and Mrs. Gorman were there too. By that hour Bill had a black eye and a split lip for his trouble. Mrs. Gorman, crazy red hair, horse teeth, and a jaw that didn't quit, was smoking like a machine and yelling at the chief of police to stick his ass in a meat grinder. Gorman's old man, with his watery eyes and drooping earlobes, stood there peering into the hole like he was contemplating maybe taking a powder himself. All I knew about him was that he crafted tiny statues from his own ear wax. I saw a yellow-brown man on horseback brandishing a sabre. He kept it in a matchbox on a piece of cotton.

All through that night, into the morning, and then through the entire next day into the night again the search continued. I overhead one of the firemen say to Mr. Torey that the sewer system beneath the school stretched out for miles in all directions, like a *labyrinth* beneath the neighborhood. That was the word he used, and when we went home, I tried to look it up in the dictionary, but I couldn't figure out how to spell it. I asked my mother when she came in to kiss me goodnight, and she said, "It means 'a maze.'" I thought she meant "amaze" not "a maze." All I saw were so many pipes going every which way for miles. It made my head spin and left me "amazed." I fell asleep with that image—a bureaucracy of sewer pipes that reached down to Hell and at the edges of their existence slowly propagated more of themselves.

Funny thing, about a month after all this happened, a miracle occurred. Mr. Boyle, the maintenance man over at Our Lady of Persistent Faith, was down in the distant third basement of that centuries-old church and heard a whimpering noise in the dark. He spun around and trained his flashlight in its direction. It appeared to be the ghost of a dog, and Mr. Boyle said the sight of it made him jump. Boyle was also a volunteer fireman, and as he got closer to the dog he recognized it to be Porkchops. All the creature's hair had turned pure white. After he was taken to the fire station, it was discovered the dog had gone blind. He was very weak and could barely get up to go outside. He died a few days later and was buried with full honors. My father decided Porkchops must have survived "on a steady diet of mice and turds."

"But why'd all his fur turn white?" I asked.

"Some crazy shit," said the old man, shrugged, and went back to reading the *Telegraph.*

By then pretty much everybody had forsaken the vigil and all hope of ever seeing the lost boy again. Only Bill religiously went to Sewer Pipe Hill and called into the big dark hole, always threatening, hoping for an answer. During that winter, I tried to figure why David Gorman had crawled out of our lives. My mother said of him, "That kid was never right." He was quiet, one of those people who couldn't look you in the eye but just give you a bashful glance every now and then. He blushed deeply and chewed on the skin of his thumb knuckle. My father said he caught him one day, knocking his head repeatedly against the wall of the Gorman's house. They lived next door to us. "He was really banging it," my father said. "His fucking head must be like a coconut." David got in trouble back in fifth grade, 'cause he showed his dick to Regina Manzo at recess one afternoon. She kicked him right in the nuts. It turned into a big deal. Torey had Mr. and Mrs. Gorman in and the cops showed up at school. He got beaten black and blue with a strap by his father and was suspended for three days.

My brother had a theory he laid out for me one night when we sat on the southern slope of Sewer Pipe Hill, looking up at the stars. He smoked a cigarette he'd stolen from my mother. The sun had just set and there was a strong cold breeze sweeping across the school fields and through the rattling autumn leaves. "So he crawls in and keeps going," said my brother, getting ready to launch into his explanation, but I stopped him by asking, "Why?" He sighed, shook his head, and then continued. "So, he's deep underground, and I'll bet you he hooks up with the mole men."

"The mole men?" I said.

"Of course."

"Which mole men? The ones with a load in their pants, bug eyes, and a zipper in the back of their dirt skin suits? Or the dwarf ones that showed up on *Superman*—ass heads with a ring of hair like Julius Caesar?"

"The real mole men, with snouts and claws for fingers," he said. "Not that fake stuff. He probably took over down there and is ruling the mole kingdom, inventing hot dogs and racing cars, machine-guns and sunglasses. He's got a mole queen and an army."

"David Gorman?"

"Just being human makes him king, right?

"So, what's he doing?"

"Planning a revolt against the surface. When the day comes he'll give the order and the mole men and women and children and their pet dogs will spill up into this world, eat everyone's faces, and turn everything you know and love into dirt."

My brother's theory seemed a sign that we'd thought too much about the disappearance. And then, all at once, the mystifying idea of the escapade seeped out of everybody's minds like old air out of a basketball in December. We went back to the reality we had before David left his conundrum in our lives. I'd pretty much forgotten it. Only when I was passing by Sewer Pipe Hill in the dark on my way home for dinner did the memory of the weird event spark a burst of adrenalin and set me running scared all the way home. Ignorance was bliss until the week before Christmas when Regina Manzo whispered to me at lunch. "Come over today, I have to show you something." The brushing of her warm words against my earlobe made it hard to swallow.

Dizzy with curiosity, I went directly to Regina's house after school. When I rang the bell, she answered and waved me in.

"Is it OK with your mother?" I asked.

Regina took my hand and led me upstairs. "My parents aren't home," she said.

"What about Lorel?" My heart had started pounding from the moment she took my hand.

"She's at cello practice."

When we reached the second floor, we didn't turn at either of the bedrooms, but headed like a beeline for the bathroom at the end of the hall. I was blushing; my breathing was jittery. She pulled me inside and shut the door behind us. My legs trembled, and I wondered if she was going to make me watch her take a piss or something. She moved in close to me as if we were gonna kiss, but she was simply reaching around me to get to the light switch. She flicked it on and the place lit up so bright I squinted. Brushing past me, she went to a vanity built into the wall and opened a small drawer.

"What are we doing?" I asked.

She put her finger to her lips and then pointed at the toilet as if it were listening. "Come here," she whispered.

Standing next to her, I could see the scraps of paper she was holding. Laying them out on the surface of the vanity, she quietly said, "There were a lot more, but I threw a bunch out." I leaned down to get a better look. All of them were wrinkled, and the ink was blurred as if they'd been left out in the rain. One in which the writing was still legible read, "Come be with me." Another bore a strange red blotch of a message. I pointed to it and Regina said, "It's a heart, like on Valentine's Day."

I nodded.

"They come up in the toilet after I pee."

"What?"

"I flush, and in the new clean water, a message bobs up from the dark hole. I try to snatch them out before the ink is smeared so much I can't read it. I don't know what some of them are trying to say."

"Where are they coming from?"

She silently mouthed the words DAVID GORMAN. "He's in love with me," she whispered and shook her head like an adult, in resignation and weariness.

After that, my recall of the incident goes dry, and when I try to force a memory, all I get is a jumble of faces and voices and the rush of seasons out of order. The only other curio I can add to this cabinet is that thirty years later in a bar in O'Hare Airport on the night of a blizzard when nothing was leaving the ground, I met Bill Gorman. He looked like a sadder, larger version of himself as a kid. He drank fast and hard—double Jack Daniels each go-round. When he laughed, he made the noise but remained expressionless.

I found out that Bill had become a much-sought-after make-up artist in Hollywood, which actually made a creepy kind of sense to me. I asked about his parents, and his response was, "Dead, finally." We went through the list of stuff either of us could remember from the old neighborhood. There was a lot of "Hey, remember . . . ?" He told me a few things I hadn't heard, like the fact that Lerner, in a suicide attempt, shot himself in the head but lived to eventually become a priest and that Regina Manzo owned her own tech company and was a millionaire.

Finally, I asked him, "Was there ever anything more about David?" He rubbed his head like a chimp to soothe the bad thoughts and said, "No. The rescue guys finally decided he must have just crawled into one of the hundreds of little passageways down there, got stuck and couldn't get out. They said that if you get nervous in a tight space your body tends to inflate. Scientists say it's not possible, but these guys worked underground for decades and swore to it. David got stuck, blew up, and died. Rats ate him. Rushing water washed him away.

"After I finally started making a lot of money in Hollywood, I'd go back to the neighborhood once a year. Fly from California, get a limo from JFK, go to Sewer Pipe Hill, stand in front of the hole and call for David. It was my yearly tribute to my brother. That only lasted until the development went up, and I got caught standing in someone's backyard one night yelling into the dark where a hole used to be. The cops came and I almost got arrested. Luckily one of them was the Weeze, and he remembered me and David. He was thin and wasted and his skin was leathery. like he'd been preserved somehow. You ever seen those Peruvian mummies? Who knows how old he was."

I pictured the Weeze's gaze still shifting but now more slowly, like the pendulum of a grandfather clock. Bill drained his drink. After ordering another, he told me, "You know, Weeze put a paw on my shoulder, patted my back, and said, 'That's all gone now. It hardly exists anymore. Once you let go, it'll be like it never happened.'"

There was much more to this story, though. I can't tell you what it was specifically, I just have a feeling that there was much more. Those parts that are lost to me passed their sell-by-date and my memory unceremoniously tossed them like gray chopped meat from the fridge. Whatever you see here is what I have left. Before I gave Bill my best and fled across the terminal, I asked him why he thought David had done it. "Was he escaping or searching for something?" I said.

He thought for a long time and gave me a heartfelt answer, but, wouldn't you know it, I've forgotten what he told me. It was one of the two options I'd offered, I think, but which? It was so frustrating trying to remember. I spent years leaning toward *escape* and then switched for a decade toward *a search,* only to realize I just couldn't definitively remember what he'd said. A sad thought, like a sour note from Lorel Manzo's long-silenced cello—in another five years or so, what's left of the story will have completely decomposed, fizzed away, fallen back into a big dark hole.

Thanksgiving

Five people sat around a dining room table in the glow of the overhead lamp while outside in the dark a light snow fell. The remains of Thanksgiving dinner had not been cleared, but merely pushed back. The group was into second coffees and slices of pumpkin pie. There was a sixth seat at the table but it was empty, though the plate of turkey bones, an abandoned sweet potato, and a few scattered pearl onions were proof it had but recently been vacated.

The old woman, Fran, with steel-gray braids wrapped in a spiral on her head, sipped at a hazelnut liqueur. "That was a great feast, Will," she said to her son-in-law.

Will, in a white shirt, sleeves rolled up, leaned back, his hands clasped behind his head, and smiled.

"I rank it as your second best effort," said Tina. "Nothing beats that one you did last year."

"My favorite too," said Will. "Deep-frying's dangerous business, though. I'm never gonna do that again."

His wife, Sue, sitting across from him, said, "Every year's a winner for me. It means I don't have to do it."

"People make a big deal out of Thanksgiving dinner, but it really is easy to prepare. I mean, I wouldn't want to have to cook for a throng of people like Sue used to, but, you know. As long as you can put shit in the oven and take it out on time, it's not much of a mystery," said Will.

Sue pushed her long red hair back from her face and said, "Hear, hear."

"How would you rank this one, Jerum?" Tina asked her husband.

"Oh, awesome. What the heck? Thanksgiving dinner's always a hit with me."

Will thanked everyone and took a drink of coffee.

Jerum then pointed his fork, holding a skewered bite of pie, at the empty seat across the table from him. "How did you all think Uncle Jake looked tonight?"

"Tired," said Tina.

"Gray," said Sue.

"Somewhat withered. Is he a drinker?" asked Fran.

"Did you notice when he stood to go home, he staggered a little? The act of putting his jacket on seemed to drain him," said Jerum.

"He's such a quiet guy. He was here all afternoon and I don't think I got three words out of him," said Will.

"I talked a little bit to him," said Sue. "He was telling me about . . . What was it? A pet armadillo? Is that possible?"

"I guess so," said Jerum, "but..."

"You know they're responsible for spreading leprosy," said Sue.

"Good lord," said Fran. "Who'd want that?"

"He told me he found five dollars in his pajama bottoms three weeks ago," said Tina. "He didn't smile when he told me. He said it flat like the words were just soft noises he was making."

Will laughed at Tina's description. "Look, don't get mad at me, because I know I should know the answer to this, but I don't think I ever knew. Whose uncle is Uncle Jake anyway?"

"We thought he was your uncle," said Tina, placing her hand softly on top of Jerum's forearm.

"I thought he was related to one of you guys," Sue said to the couple.

"That's what I assumed," said Will.

"He's not in our family, is he?" Sue asked Fran.

"Not that I'm aware of."

"Are you sure you guys didn't bring him to one of those Thanksgivings back when there'd be fifty people here?" asked Will.

Tina and Jerum shook their heads. She said, "The first time I ever saw him was back about fifteen years ago here. The place was packed and he introduced himself to me as Uncle Jake. He had a plate of food in his hand and was moving slowly through the crowd. He was kind of beat looking even back then. I remember thinking at the time he might not be all there."

"I remember the same," said Jerum. "I've talked to him through the years, but I'll be damned if I remember anything he's told me. Oh, except that he lives behind the Stop and Shop off of Currier."

"You mean you've had him to Thanksgiving dinner for fifteen years and nobody knew who he was?" asked Fran. "That's ridiculous."

"He must be related to somebody we knew who used to come to the earlier dinners," said Will. "I recall the first one that I cooked four years ago after Sue gave up on the big melees. I got in touch with everyone in January to give them plenty of time to plan and told them that we wouldn't be having a huge affair that year or anymore to come. So when he showed up at the door that Thanksgiving, I figured he just didn't get the memo. And I was like, Uncle Jake? What the hell. He doesn't eat much. But then he kept coming back every year, and I didn't have the heart to ditch him."

"Kind of creepy," said Tina.

"Kind of," said Sue.

"I see this guy once in a while on the street, you know, maybe two, three times a year. I see him passing on the sidewalk, always dressed in that saggy blue serge suit. It's like, 'Hi, Uncle Jake.' I shake his hand, he mumbles some bullshit about Thanksgiving dinner, and he's on his way. His conversational repertoire is slim," said Jerum.

"God, that suit," said Will. "Every year without fail, that suit. It looks like he got worked over in it."

"I always thought he was a greasy dude," said Tina.

"I just thought he was lonely, like his wife had died some years earlier and it made him withdraw from life," said Sue.

"That's what I thought," said Jerum. "Tina thought he was a perv from the word go."

"You know," said Will, "the other reason I never really questioned Uncle Jake's Thanksgiving visits was because, with the exception of Fran, we don't have any older relatives still living. It's nice around the holiday time to have that connection to the past."

"I guess I can see that," said Jerum, "but if I run into him on the street tomorrow, I'm gonna hide."

"I don't want him here anymore," Sue said to Will. "He could be dangerous."

"After fifteen years you think he's gonna suddenly make his move? You could put him down with a pipe cleaner. He's harmless. Besides, I have a feeling he still might be related to one of us but we just aren't aware of it."

"That doesn't make any fuckin' sense," said Sue.

"I know," said Will. "I could hear that as I was saying it."

"But what *do* you remember about him?" asked Tina. She reached into her purse and pulled out a pad and pen. "We should make a list."

After that, they all just spoke out their tidbits of memory and Tina took them down, carefully printing each word and using hearts to dot the *i*'s.

"The only consistent theme to the sad-ass conversations I've had with him through the years," said Will, "was the end of the world. He could talk the apocalypse like a door-to-door dust salesman. He'd spill the horrors in that drawl straight from dreamland and I'd listen, bored bone stiff."

"Say you only got three words to describe Uncle Jake. What would they be?" asked Tina.

"At least one would be 'turnip,'" said Jerum.

"Damaged," said Sue.

"There you are," said Tina. "He's a damaged, threatening turnip."

"In a blue serge suit," added Jerum.

"That does kind of nail it," said Will.

"OK," said Tina. "What movie star does he look like?"

"Kind of a cross between Shemp from the Stooges and John Caradine in a cardigan sweater," said Jerum.

"You're on the right track," said Will, "but I'm thinking more Basil Rathbone meets Willem Dafoe. You know, really run down and pale, under the spell of gravity."

Jerum nodded in agreement.

"Pretty good," said Sue, "but there's one ingredient missing. I'm down with everything said so far, but you have to agree the mix needs more than just a sprinkling of Robert Duvall's Boo Radley."

They all agreed but for Fran, who saw Uncle Jake more like a dim-witted, arthritic Andy Griffith. "It's not a good idea to ignore aspects of the supernatural like we have here," said Fran.

"No one's talking supernatural," said Tina. "I'm thinkin' sad loser hears a party going on, a Thanksgiving dinner, while walking by in the street one day some fifteen years ago. He goes into the party and joins it, not in his own name, but passing himself off as Uncle Jake. Since he's a sad sack, he's got nothing to do so he decides to return every year, and it happens that you two are the Thanksgiving couple."

Sue nodded in agreement and said, "I do remember him once telling me 'The gaucho laughs in your mirror.'"

"What's that?" asked Will.

"I don't know," said Sue. "We were in the living room and it was crowded, people everywhere. Food hadn't been served and everybody was getting loose. The Ronettes were on Pandora. I saw him slip through the crowd like a thought. Before I knew it, he was beside me and saying in that see-ya-later tone, 'The gaucho laughs in your mirror.'"

"What ever the fuck that means," said Fran.

"I know," said Sue, laughing.

"Forget him," said Jerum. "You've got till next year to consider what you're gonna do."

"What if we just let him in and let him join us for dinner," said Will, "like he does every year, and he won't know we know, but we'll all know the depths of his weirdness?"

"I don't think I could keep a straight face through that," said Sue.

"What do you say would happen if he suddenly came to the realization that we all knew he was nobody's uncle? I mean like right in the middle of Thanksgiving dinner?" asked Jerum.

"A killing rampage?" said Fran.

"The earth would swallow him like Rumpelstiltskin," said Tina.

With that, they all breathed a sigh of relief. There was another round of the hazelnut liqueur and Uncle Jake was forgotten about until mid-September. It was Tina who mentioned it first. She called Sue on the day she noticed the leaves turning red and reminded her about Thanksgiving and Uncle Jake.

"Oh, yeah, I tried to forget that whole thing."

"Well, you've got two months till he'll be tapping at your door."

When Sue reminded Will about Uncle Jake, he said, "It's on my mind. It haunts me at night sometimes. I think what we need to do is have Thanksgiving out somewhere. He'll tap on the door and eventually figure that we're onto him or that something happened to Thanksgiving. Either way I don't care. I just don't want to deal with him."

"I thought you were the one who wanted to let him in and play along that we didn't know anything about his deception."

"Hot air," he said.

"Run away is the answer?" said Sue.

"Definitely," said Will. "Got a better idea?"

So they rented the party room at the back of a local restaurant, The Colonel's Wife. It was an old place with a history. The Colonel's Wife was supposedly a woman from the Revolutionary War who tended an inn on the premises and poisoned a dinner's party worth of Brits. It was a basic steak and potatoes place with candlelight and a well-stocked wine cellar. The room the five were ushered into was decorated with strings of bright yellow leaves recently fallen from the giant oaks in the library field across the street.

Fran was dressed in a pale blue-green gown that seemed cut from a waterfall. In her hair she wore a very delicate tiara made of looped wire. She told Sue and Tina about her trip to the snake mound in October. They nodded like they were interested, but both of them found Fran a little affected, although they still loved her.

Jerum sloughed off his coat and handed it to the young woman who'd ushered them through the restaurant proper, through the mists of roast turkey and oyster dressing, to the back room. Once she was gone and they'd each taken a seat at the long table, he said, "You didn't say a thing about this but I knew when you called to switch Thanksgiving from your place to here that it was in order to avoid Uncle Jake." He laughed.

"Guilty as charged," said Will.

"Three days ago," said Jerum, "I was walking home from the train, thinking about Thanksgiving Dinner, about having it here. I was looking forward to the event. In the next instant, Uncle Jake was in front of me with his hand extended. His presence shocked me because just that morning I found out from you that we were meeting at the Colonel's Wife. When I looked up to greet him, there was a real energy in his stare. He clasped my hand tightly so that I couldn't back away. He talked a string of bullshit about Thanksgiving. I mean head-spinning stuff. Then he gripped my hand yet tighter, widened his eyes, and said 'See you there' before moving on."

"Did he seem to know we were gonna stiff him?" asked Sue.

"I couldn't tell," said Jerum. "It did feel as if he could look right into my head and know I'd lied to him. He was dreadfully run down. Creeping along the sidewalk. Smelled like bad milk. But his grip was extraordinary. It was like he was flexing his wrinkles. Otherworldly."

"We'll stay extra late," said Fran, "and he'll be gone by the time you get back home. I doubt he'll sleep on your steps or anything like that."

"I'll tell him to fuck off," said Will.

"That's not necessary," said Sue.

Then the wait staff appeared with cocktails and the Thanksgiving dinner got into full swing. The appetizer was fried mozzarella and slices of pear and apple. Tina and Jerum sat on the left side of the table, next to each other, and both ordered a double gin with an ice cube. Fran sat across from Will, and Sue sat at the head of the table. All three of them had red wine. The room, though long, was also fairly wide, the walls covered ceiling to floor with fading black and white photographs in cheap black frames. At each corner there was a nest of lit candles sitting on a high stool. There were no windows and plenty of shadows.

The appetizer had been cleared and they awaited bowls of cream of mutton soup with lentils and rutabaga. There was a brief pause in the cross talk and Tina said, "Did any of you notice?" She was pointing down to the end of the table opposite Sue, where there was another place setting.

"How many diners did you tell them?" asked Fran.

Will held his hand up, fingers splayed. "Five. That's all."

After the soup course, from everywhere at once there came a persistent banging sound. There was a brief pause and then it resumed, almost like a code. They all looked up and around and into the shadows. Will finally left his seat and went into the darkness behind Sue's chair at the very back of the room. "There's a door here," he called. They heard him open it, and the slanting red sun of a cold dusk shot into the room and gave the place the sense of a tractor trailer being opened at its destination. All at the table heard Will say, "Oh, Uncle Jake, glad you could make it."

From the table came the whispered word, "Shit."

The diners heard the door in the dark close and watched as Uncle Jake staggered into view. In his blue suit, he passed down the length of the table to his seat, without making eye contact with any of them. His hands shook and he wheezed. Upon sitting, he said, "Thanksgiving, yeah, you know, OK?" chuckled good-naturedly and then stared at his plate. Will crept back to his seat. Drinks were drained in silence. Tina looked at Jerum, who looked at Will, who stared at Sue while Fran watched all of them.

"You missed the cream of mutton, Uncle Jake," said Will.

Two seconds passed and then Sue burst out laughing.

Uncle Jake looked nervously from one of them to the next and slowly lifted his butter knife.

Fran yelled, "He's an entity. Deny his existence if you want to live."

"Uncle Jake," said Jerum, "we know you're nobody's uncle."

"Tell him he's a dilapidated sack of shit," said Fran. When no one responded, she yelled, "Tell him."

Will blurted out, "You're a dilapidated sack of shit."

"Oh, sure," said Uncle Jake. "You know me and so forth. Go ahead. Happy Thanksgiving and all. Pass the pearl onions."

"You're a liar and a creep, Uncle Jake."

"I heard that before once when the weather was warmer. You know how it goes and so forth. Sure. I mean, why not?"

"Where's your home?" asked Tina.

"On the corner of Currier where it runs behind the Stop and Shop," said Uncle Jake, nodding.

"I went and checked, and Currier doesn't run anywhere near the Stop and Shop," she said.

That's when it became evident that Uncle Jake was melting, his flesh like hot wax. All the time he sloughed himself in bright rivulets, he mumbled random snatches of Thanksgiving pleasantries and inanities, and profanities. His chin became his fists and his eyeballs slid down the melting mass of his body to the floor. His last words before his head caved in entirely and became one with the rest of whatever he was becoming were, "Sure, sure. You know. Absolutely!"

All five of them stood and gathered around Uncle Jake's steaming chair.

"What the fuck happened to him?" asked Sue.

"We denied his existence," said Fran.

"Rough justice," said Tina, holding her nose with thumb and index finger.

"He stinks like melted Uncle Jake," said Jerum.

"The waiters are gonna come in here and think we all pitched in and shit on this chair," said Will.

"Let's get out of here," said Tina. She grabbed her coat from a hook near the front of the room and grabbed Will's and Sue's and Fran's as well. Jerum, wearing a cardigan sweater, left his jacket behind. She led the way into the darkness behind Sue's chair, found the door, and pushed through it. The hinges gave a squeal. Night had fallen while they were melting Uncle Jake. Each went immediately to their respective cars and left the parking lot.

Eventually the restaurant caught up with Will and Sue, who erased the problem of the ruined chair by throwing money at it. The owner of the Colonel's Wife told Sue on the phone, after all the details had been worked out and the bill had been paid, that she and her party would no longer be welcome in the establishment.

"Solid," said Sue and hung up.

Although they all seemed free of Uncle Jake, they didn't feel as if they were. No one was satisfied with his demise. All had misgivings, but more importantly all had theories of what he was and where he'd come from. Nothing about the affair made sense and so they clutched fiercely to their individual explanations.

Fran, of course, was certain Uncle Jake was an evil entity, the kind her guru had warned her about. Some kind of manifested demon of middle-class rage gone mute. She would never accept the argument that he melted of his own volition.

Sue talked it over with Will on New Year's Eve as they got slowly plastered on whiskey sours. "I'm betting he was a ghost of someone who had once lived in this house," she said.

"I never thought of that," said Will. "I'll ask around the neighborhood and see if any of the old-timers remember anyone dying here." Both he and Sue did that for the next few months whenever they'd see someone out shoveling snow or working in the garden when the weather got warmer. Almost all of their older neighbors told them that there was a pet dog who lived there that passed away in its sleep one day. "Nice dog, a big black Lab/Shepard mix" said the woman next door. "Was its name, Jake?" asked Sue. "No, Shadow," said the neighbor.

Jerum fretted the least about it. His theory revolved around the idea that Uncle Jake was only ever half there, that he'd come together from the thoughts of the Thanksgiving crowds of the earlier parties and, more or less, "stayed too long at the fair." When Tina told him his explanation didn't add up, he shrugged and said, "At least I won't have to see that asshole on the street anymore."

It took Tina a long time to come to her own understanding. Two years after that last Thanksgiving at the Colonel's Wife, the last she and Jerum shared with Will and Sue and Fran, she woke from a dead sleep one night with the idea rattling in her head that the five of them were merely ancillary characters in a world whose center was Uncle Jake. It had all always been about him and they'd missed it. When he melted before them, they never perceived that he was blowing them off, abandoning them to a shell of a reality he no longer had use for. And truth be told, since he was gone, the world had lost focus and fire—a plate of turkey bones, a cold sweet potato, a few pearl onions.

Five-Pointed Spell

The Black Pickup

I was freshly moved from South Jersey to the farm country of Ohio in the midst of a frozen February, 2012. I'd given up my job, my friends, my close proximity to New York City, to the shore, so that Lynn could have her dream job.

We had a big hundred-plus-year-old farmhouse out in the middle of nothing but corn and soybean fields. The property had a fruit-tree orchard, some land for a big garden, and a few acres of fields off to the side, separating us from the farm next door. There was a little shed just beyond the kitchen door and, at the end of a fifty-yard driveway, a big old hangar of a garage.

In the midst of winter, the place was desolate. The fields, as far as the eye could see, were a stubble of harvested stalks and perpetually overcast. Frigid wind sliced across the emptiness and late at night I sometimes heard whispering although everyone else was asleep.

Lynn was off at work all day, and I was home doing nothing. I was supposed to be writing, supposed to be searching online for another teaching gig. In fact, dozing was my thing. The place sapped my consciousness. Any task was too much for me except going to the kitchen to make sandwiches. The other thing I did a lot of was put my sweatshirt and coat on and go out on the porch to smoke a couple of cigarettes and stare off into the distance across the empty fields.

Eventually I ran out of cigarettes and had to get dressed like a human being, not just shorts and a T-shirt, and go out in the car. I remember that's just what I did, actually happy to have a mission. It was around one in the afternoon. I pulled out of the driveway in my CRV and headed east. Town was eleven miles away, and to get there I had to take narrow, impossibly straight roads lined with telephone poles spaced out judiciously to mark infinity.

I rarely passed a car coming or going. The deep country was a place I'd always wanted to live until I actually did. There was a peregrine falcon on the telephone wire, and off across an empty field I saw the hunched forms of two coyotes. For some reason I looked up into my rear view mirror, and there was a black pick-up truck right on my ass.

Tailgating wasn't the word for it. I had no idea where it'd come from. I'm not a brave driver or a fast driver to begin with, and I was unfamiliar with the roads, which made me more leery. Besides there was still a rime of ice on the cracked asphalt from a snowstorm two days earlier.

I did what I always did when I encountered a sudden problem driving; I slammed on the brakes. Not a great idea. I don't know how the truck didn't hit me. The high beams flashed on and off and the horn blared. In my rearview mirror, I saw a hulking figure behind the wheel. My inclination was to give him the finger, but the last thing I needed was to be run off the road and beaten senseless by some corn-fed hodunk. I pulled slowly over to the side, and he flew past me, horn blaring. Once he was out of sight, I started again for town.

At the convenience store, I bought a couple of packs of butts and a twleve-pack of beer for that night. Driving down the main street, I looked around to see if the black truck was parked anywhere. The town is small, three tanning salons, a closed bank, a dive bar, a gas station, the convenience store, and a little park where they had a yearly ox roast that attracted more flies than people.

I looked everywhere for the truck. I'm not sure what I expected to do if I found it. Luckily, no luck. I headed back home, window cracked halfway, smoking a cig and daydreaming about breaking into the beers and smoking a joint on the porch that night. Every once in a while, I peered up at my rearview mirror just to see that the coast was clear,

I was about halfway home when off in the far distance of that long straight road I spotted a vehicle moving swiftly, gaining speed on me. "No way," I said aloud and pushed down on the accelerator a bit. I looked up again to see if I could make out the model of car. It had drawn close enough for me to see that it wasn't a car at all but a pickup truck. "Fuck," I said, and in that instant it took for me to say it, it had become clear that not only was it a truck but it was a black truck.

He must have been doing 90 on that poopy country road. I pushed down on the gas, to my mind, recklessly, but as wild as I thought I was driving, I didn't stand a chance of outpacing him. I looked at the speedometer and I was only doing 55. "Jesus," I said, threw the butt out the window and closed it. I inched up to 60 mph but felt as if the car was getting out of control. Then the truck was right behind me, flashing its lights and beeping.

I pulled over at almost exactly the spot I'd pulled over on the way to town. My heart was pounding, and as I hit the brakes to coast to the side, the car wriggled erratically. A dark blur blew past me and I saw the guy in the driver's seat. He stared over at me with a dull expression while chewing on a cigar that looked like a piece of black rope. One detail I caught as he whipped out of sight was that under his orange cap in the back, the hair had been shaved from his scalp behind his ear and there was a big white Frankenstein scar like his head had been stitched back on. It matched up somehow in my mind with the decal on his back window—a spear point with a sword in it and lightning bolts shooting across it like scars.

For the next few weeks, every time I left the house, I'd warily check my rearview mirror, and not once was it in vain. That guy had to be spying on me. I asked the farmers on either side of my place if they knew who it was, describing the truck to them. Both of them more or less said the same thing, "Oh, yeah, that black truck, I've seen it before."

I had no idea if it came from in the direction of town or west, where I pictured things were that much staler than where we lived. I asked around at the diner and convenience store if anybody recognized the vehicle. Then about three weeks after my first encounter with the pickup, I went out to get butts and couldn't believe it when I'd made it all the way to Main Street in town without being tailgated. What a relief. The way back home, the same.

Days passed. A couple of weeks passed, and I saw neither hide nor hair of my nemesis. I figured he'd probably gotten fed up with me because I wasn't about to race him, and I certainly wasn't going to pull over and fight him. I could live with the shame.

A Cold Notion

The stories were starting to congeal between my ears, and I desperately needed some fresh air and exercise. I decided to hitch up the dog and drive over to this enormous piece of parkland not that far from our house. It was partially on the way to town but then a left and a trip down a two-mile straight road and then a right. The place was empty in the cold end of February. Sometimes, in the late afternoon, Fin the dog and I were the only ones there.

As much as I was down on Ohio, the landscape of this area was beautiful and varied. There was a lake that we could walk around; there was a place where they'd restored a few hundred acres to its original prairie state. There was a trail through the woods along a creek that as far as we'd followed it, it just kept on going. Those walks did a lot to start to bring me around, and we went religiously, seeing as there was nothing else to do.

One gray afternoon, early in March, we went to the park as usual. It was still freezing, colder than it had been in days. We made our usual transit around the lake and were heading for the parking lot when, just before we left the trail, I thought I heard the sound of someone's voice. Fin stopped short and peered down the embankment where it led through the trees to the lake. As I approached I heard the voice distinctly over the wind. I sidled up and looked down. The sight startled me. There was a guy down there, his back to me. His head was cocked to the side like he might have known we were looking at him but he didn't want to make full-on eye contact. He was talking to himself or praying or something, and then I saw the gun barrel next to his leg. He was holding a rifle.

I pulled Fin by the leash and double-timed it as fast as my bubble butt could carry me back to the parking lot. When I came through the trees and saw my car, I noticed the black pickup was parked a few spots over from it, the only two vehicles in the lot. We got in the car and split. As I pulled out of the lot, I saw the driver emerging from the woods. In my flight, I tried to identify him as the same guy who'd passed me on the road. For a moment, I was certain of it but grew less so the nearer I got to home.

Later it struck me that I might have smelled traces of that short black cigar on the breeze—an aroma somewhere between a horse blanket and the dark back part of a closet. The wind was blowing a clip that day, though, and I'm not sure the memory was real. Fin and I stayed away from the park for a few weeks, but eventually I really needed to get out, and the weather had gotten much nicer as spring came on.

With enough distance in time, I was willing to chalk up the driver with the gun as just a product of my paranoia. I wondered if that's what I'd really seen. Most days I didn't interact with anyone except Lynn when she got home late at night from work. Anyway, there were a lot of people at the park with the better weather, so Fin and I returned. It felt great to get back to walking, and there was no sign of the pickup on the road or in the parking lot.

All through the end of March and into April and May we traipsed every inch of that park, building strength and health. One afternoon, making our way through a light drizzle along the stream, deeper and deeper into the woods than we'd ever been before, we came upon something on the ground set off from the bank a few yards. I'd not have seen it if there hadn't been at that bend a number of large, orange-hued toadstools dotting the ground. I followed them to where they were thickest, and there, in an obviously constructed stone circle, I found evidence of a recent fire.

At the center of the pile of blackened ash were the bones of some animal formed into a teepee with the skull, that of maybe a dog or fox or coyote, sitting atop the teepee point. Smoke still curled up through the empty eye holes. The smell was sharp and sent a cold notion creeping up my spine. *A sacrifice?* I wondered. *Some kind of ritual?* My ears did that prehistoric thing when suddenly they prick up to listen for trouble.

I spun slowly around and looked everywhere to see if someone was watching me. Fin whined a little and walked a circle around me as if to herd me back to moving. On the ground, just outside the ring of stones, I saw a few half-smoked black cigars. I don't know why I did it, but before I left the scene, I stepped into the ring of stones and kicked over the bones and skull. They clattered in every direction. And then we ran along the stream. We saw no one. Upon our return home, I felt exhilarated. Something about my insinuating myself into the remains of that ritual site energized me. That night, for the first time since I'd moved to Ohio, I went back to writing.

Pow-Wow

Having grown up on Long Island and lived in Jersey, the kinds of rituals I was used to were coffee and cigarettes in the morning while reading the newspaper, going to the bar Friday nights. I'd never been part of anything where animals were being sacrificed and burned, unless you count my old man's barbecues.

There was a large Pennsylvania Dutch influence in Ohio. More Amish settled in Ohio than in Pennsylvania. The "Dutch" part of the equation didn't mean these folks were from Holland; it meant they were from Germany—Deutch. The language group was Low German and some of them practiced a kind of ritualistic magic tied to the earth. Much of it probably began as a pagan religion in Europe and then was subsumed by the coming of Christianity. I read up on hex magic.

Supposedly it still survived in the area from Pennsylvania throughout Ohio and into Indiana. It dealt with the elements, the weather, the power of the earth. There were entities that needed cajoling and adepts that needed consultation if you wanted to work a curse on someone or set a charm to help a friend out of a bind. I was surprised that so much of it still existed. It took a little looking, but I found a real hex doctor nearby and went to visit. My meeting with the old man wasn't cheap. From what I'd read online he was the real deal, though.

Averal Braun lived two towns over, back in the woods in an old house you'd miss a hundred times driving by on the road. He gave me a whole protocol to follow before I came to see him, so that no evil spirits followed me or something like that. The acts I was to perform seemed ridiculous, and I was sworn not to discuss them.

I had a sit down with him for the better part of an hour on his screened-in porch. He was a hard guy to read—a strict demeanor when composed but easy to laugh. His hairdo was munchkin-like—tufts erupting from the top and sides of his head. He wore old-fashioned spectacles with round lenses and wire arms.

There were certain things I asked him that he said he couldn't answer, but he was forthcoming as to a lot of the history of the rituals and tradition, the nature of some of the symbols used. He had a lot of great local stories from the time he was a boy and the magic was more widely practiced—a corrupt physician taken by a death fetch, a woman who burst into flames, talking animals, and love charms galore.

The one thing he was emphatic about was that I not dig too deeply into it. I told him I might want to use the subject of it in a story, and he said that would probably be OK, as long as I was vague and didn't name names or give away spells. "You don't want to anger someone who really knows what they're doing with this, though," he said and nodded slowly. His prominent Adam's apple bobbed up and down like a third eye taking me in through a scrim of throat flesh.

"You know, Mr. Ford," he said. "There's a big difference as to how the supernatural operates in storybooks and real life. You say you're a writer."

I nodded.

"In real life, the supernatural declines to explain. In fiction, it must. I'm not talking about sleight of hand by some clever magus. I mean events that are truly supernatural. In those cases, the storyline runs deeper than most are willing to dive."

I came out with my story about the stone circle and the sacrificed animal. When I told him, the first thing he asked me is what kind of animal it was that had been killed. I told him either a fox, a dog, or a coyote, and then asked him if it made a difference. He shook his head and muttered "Nah," although it was clear that it did. He had me tell him where precisely the stone circle had been in the woods, and I did my best. He seemed interested in the giant orange mushrooms that dotted the site.

"Do you have any enemies?" he asked.

"Not that I'm aware of. But I do have a hunch that the guy who killed that creature is the same guy who had been following me in his pickup truck."

"Following you?"

I explained.

"You'd never seen him before?"

"Never saw him till that first day in February when I pulled out of my driveway. I hadn't done anything to him."

"Wait a second," said the old man. "What do you mean by you hadn't? Have you since?"

"Well, I scattered his bone pile, but . . ."

I quit talking because Braun took a comb out of the pocket of his flannel shirt and slapped it three times against the back of his left wrist. "Listen, Mr. Ford," he said. "You can't think of those operating in spellwork and Pow-Wow as if they're tied to the regular passage of time or its perceived effects. You understand?"

"Nonlinear?"

He put the comb back in his shirt pocket, clapped his hands, and pointed at me. "You got it."

"So he might have been harassing me on the road because I wrecked his bone pile, even though my wrecking the bone pile came after his harassing me?"

Braun nodded. "But you know, it could all mean something else entirely. It could have to do with something that hasn't even happened yet. Speak no more about it now. Take this," he said and handed me an everyday object (he said if I told anyone about it, it'd lose its power to protect me). "Keep that on you all the time. Go home now and don't be thinking about Pow-Wow for a while. Write about something else. I got a protection charm at work. Be wary of anyone who seems cockeyed to you. Don't have any business with them. I'll send somebody by to check up on you in a while. A day might come, after this is resolved, when you'll realize what it was about. The pieces will fly together."

Of course I was more intrigued than ever, but the old guy scared the crap out of me. I was about as fearless against the supernatural as I was driving over fifty. I kept the whole thing out of my mind and wrote a story set in Japan. Half the time I thought Braun was pulling my leg, but still, when I'd get up in the middle of the night to take a piss, I'd peer out the bedroom window to see if the black truck was parked in front of the house.

I wanted to tell Lynn, but I was sworn to secrecy, and the whole thing was just getting way too complicated to describe.

Stranger in the Orchard

I had story deadlines, and I'd picked up a few classes a semester at a liberal arts university about forty-five minutes away. Life was starting to fill up with Ohio. I didn't have much time for the park, but when Fin and I did go we'd stay away from the creek through the woods and stick to the lake or prairie. It was mid-July, still and hot, and I didn't give a damn about hexes and spells; I was too busy praying that the air conditioner would keep running till October.

Off from teaching, I consumed a lot of wine by moonlight on the porch. I'd sit out there with Lynn and a couple of bottles, a candle going, watching the fireflies across the field next to the house. She usually fell asleep somewhere around 11:00, and I'd wake her to go up to bed, and then I'd sit there and rock and smoke and drink into the following morning. The sunrises, I heard, were beautiful, and Lynn would send me photos of the dawn she'd snapped before heading out to work, but I never witnessed one as I'd usually climbed into bed just as the birds began to sing. The clouds of the afternoon were towering palaces of cotton, ships heading out to sea.

On a Monday afternoon in late July, I was sitting out in the orchard. There was a warm breeze blowing across the fields and filtering into shadows beneath the trees. There were trace scents of apple and pear. I could see the clear blue sky through the leaves and hear the insects in the garden. I had my iPad on a stand and a keyboard and was writing a story about a local museum I'd recently visited.

The hair on the back of my neck stood up and the goosebumps gave me a shiver. I turned around in my chair and looked behind me. There stood a tall young woman with bangs, mid-length hair, and a jaw as wide as my forehead. She was dressed in some old-time pink dress as if fashioned from a cotton feed sack.

"Well?" I said. I looked at Fin, who was standing there quietly sniffing her shoes, and thought thanks for the warning, buddy.

She pushed her glasses up the bridge of her nose with her free hand. In the other was a metal detector and a metal shovel. "Hello, sir. Sorry to bother you. My name is Sylvia Benet, and I'm a graduate history student at Ohio State University. I'm involved in a project where we are going to some of the older properties in the area and doing shallow metal searches for everyday objects of the past, old coins, etc."

"You want to look around in my yard?"

"This place has been here a hundred years, am I correct?" she asked.

"Over a hundred," I said. "Go ahead and look around."

"I'll let you know if I find anything." Fin followed behind her as she headed for the side of the house.

A while had passed and I'd given myself back up to the writing when I felt her behind me again. I turned and she stepped forward. It was as if she'd have stood there all day waiting if I'd decided not to turn. She didn't have her equipment with her but she held a strange object in her hand.

"Look what I found out in the middle of the field," she said. She laid what looked like a tree root on the table next to the keyboard. It was splayed at the bottom into a Y, and at the other end there was a bulbous knot with crude facial features etched into it and rusted metal screws for eyes. "It was the screws that let me pick it up on the detector."

"What the hell is it?" I asked.

"Some kind of homemade doll," she said.

"Creepy."

"You know, that tree in the corner of your property," she said and pointed off beyond the garage.

"The white oak?" I asked.

"Yes. That's a very famous landmark around here, or at least it was back in the day. It's a stunning tree."

"A landmark?" I said.

"A landmark and also involved in more than one local legend."

"Sometimes I just find myself sitting on the porch staring at it," I told her.

"Well, sorry to bother you. Just thought I'd bring that for you to see. I'm going to finish up in the front by the porch and then be on my way."

"You'll let me know if you find anything else?" I asked, but she'd already started away and I'd spoken too softly for her to hear.

I held the tree-root doll in my hands and stared out through the trees at the cornfields beyond our garden. I watched the breeze move through them while I wondered about the origins of the root. I'm not sure how long I sat like that, but eventually I put the thing aside and got back to work. I'd decided if the girl wanted to take the thing with her for school, I'd say yes.

An hour passed, and when next I looked up, I noticed that the sky had darkened considerably and that the breeze had become a wind. The storm was moving in from the west, which was the usual direction for bad weather. I knew the rain would begin to fall in seconds. I picked up my iPad and keyboard and stand, the root doll, and headed for the house. Fin was at my heels, and he barked. We made our way to the porch at the side of the house, where I set everything down on a small table and then sat and lit a cigarette.

It only struck me then that I'd not seen the student again. I got up and made my way around the porch to the front of the house. She was nowhere in sight and her car was gone. "Oh, well," I said to Fin and returned to my seat and my cigarettes. I looked across the field at the white oak. Sometimes at night, after a few wines, I could literally feel that tree breathing. Now, with the doll, obviously fashioned from an oak root, I could feel it thinking.

That night, on the porch, when I showed the doll to Lynn, she said, "That's weird."

"I know."

"Get rid of it."

"Where?"

"Throw it in the back by the cornfield, where the compost heap is. You know, the Christmas tree graveyard back there."

"You want me to just leave it there? Lurking?"

Lynn drank her wine and shut her eyes, leaning back onto her chair. There was an owl calling from the north, off in the windbreak amidst the sea of corn. "We'll have to burn it," she said.

"Rough justice."

The very next day, after a solid morning of writing, I decided in the late afternoon to cook an early dinner. Lynn wouldn't return till late and would already have eaten, so why wait? I fixed up a chicken and stuck it in the oven to bake. While it cooked, I sat at the counter in the kitchen reading Basho and there was a knock. Fin barked like mad. I shuffled over to the door in my bare feet and opened it. There was a man and woman standing on the porch. He was in his early seventies, I'd say—a shorter, rounded fellow with white hair, big lips, and a hat. She was a very tall woman with a coat and purse from my mother's era.

They were from around the bend, from a church over there. I missed whatever denomination it was. I don't think it was Baptist nor Mennonite, some Christian deal I'd never heard of. Anyway, they were very nice. We stood on the porch and chatted. I explained to them that I really appreciated them coming by but that I wasn't very religious.

"That's a shame," said the guy. "We were hoping you'd come over and visit."

"Thanks," I said, "but I don't think so." I tried to smile.

"The reason it's too bad," said the preacher's wife, "is we've got an opening for someone right now. That doesn't happen as often as you think."

"What do you mean, an opening?"

"A spot," said the preacher. "Last week this young guy who was part of the parish got himself killed in a car wreck over on the back way to town. He was run off into a ditch by a guy in a pickup."

I was slightly stunned by how enamored they'd thought I'd be of the concept of their having a "spot" for me, not to mention the surprise news of the pickup. I was struck silent.

Finally, after waiting for me to respond, the preacher said, "The cops got the driver of the truck. Oh, yeah, he's going to jail, but we've got a place for you among us."

"Was it a black pickup?" I asked.

They both nodded.

It took me a while to unload them off the porch. I endured the whole thing out of respect for their reaching out, although I found their offer, to say the least, kind of spooky. I let these concerns slip away because I had to wrap my imagination simultaneously around the fact that the black pickup had recently been hunting, and the fact that the infernal driver was now behind bars, which was a relief.

As the old couple stepped off the bottom step of the porch, she turned back and said, "The young man, from our church who passed away, he grew up as a child in your house."

"Grew up here?" I said and for some reason pointed at the boards of the porch.

They didn't answer, and they didn't look back. They got into a midsized, older-model sedan, pulled out of the driveway, and were gone. My chicken was burned, and the oak doll was missing from the table on the porch when Lynn and I stepped out for wine later that evening. There was no possible other explanation but that the pastor and his wife took off with the thing. I told Lynn and she said, "Let them have it. At least we're rid of it."

Remember Me

I got a gig doing a reading in New York City; a decent reason for escaping the cornfields and hitting the road. I decided not to take a flight but to drive to South Jersey, park the car at the Hamilton train station in the overnight lot, and get a room in the city for a few days. I figured not spending for a plane ticket would offset the expense of a hotel in the Rotten Apple.

Lynn was glad to see me get out of the house and encouraged the trip. The drive to Jersey wasn't bad. Along the way I listened to a book on tape about the making of Orson Welles's last, never-shown film, *The Other Side of the Wind.* I spent a night with my painter friend, Barney, down in Dividing Creek in South Jersey, and then stayed a night with some old neighbors who lived closer to the train station. The next morning, before sunrise, I took off for New York. I stowed my car in the parking garage and was on my way.

The place I'd booked in NYC was as cheap as I could get it—less than 200 bucks. The room was made for some smaller race of people. I had to sidle around the bed, which took up the majority of the room, stand sideways in the shower, and sort of hover over the bowl to take a shit. At some point in the middle of each of the three long nights I stayed in that room, I woke in a sweat, choking. Each time I managed to calm down and take hold of myself. The good part was that I was so busy I only inhabited the miserable hovel for a few hours per night. I had lunches with editors and my agent and saw old friends. I made visits to a few of my favorite restaurants and museums.

The evening of the reading, the last night I'd be in the city, I had an early dinner and some drinks at the B Bar on East 4th Street. The place I had to read was up 4th a few blocks, so it was convenient, plus the B Bar, at the time, had a spot outside, a patio where you could still smoke. I had a salad and a beer by myself out there on a beautiful summer evening. My manuscript was on the table, and I leisurely went through it. All was well, and I was actually looking forward to heading back to Ohio the next day.

Just as I checked my watch and saw that I only had a half hour before I'd have to head up the street to the KGB Bar, someone stepped up to my table and put their hand out as if to shake. I looked up, confused, and took in the person's face. Still, out of politeness I shook hands.

"Can I help you?" I said.

The stranger, a guy of about my age with a beard and salt and pepper, hair pulled the empty seat out across from me and sat down. "You don't remember me, do you?"

"I'm sorry," I said. "I'm getting old." But his face wasn't familiar in the least.

"Binghamton University," he said, and I nodded. I had attended undergraduate and graduate school there. I shifted my thinking.

"Writing workshop with Gardner."

That was a class and professor I'd had.

"Oh fuck it, Jeff," he said. "Toby Madduc."

The name was familiar to me, and now that it had been said, I did recognize the face, although, I suppose much like mine, it had gone through the fun-house mirror of time.

"Toby," I said. "What the hell. I'm so sorry I didn't recognize you. You actually are looking great."

"Oh, fuck, no I'm not," he said. The waitress passed by and he turned to order us beers.

"What have you been up to?" I asked.

"Just working. But hey, I've seen what you've been up to. I've read all your books and story collections, seen the reviews in the *Times*, the *LA Times*, the *Washington Post*. Awesome. You're famous." He smiled, and I couldn't tell if he was being genuine or breaking my balls.

"Yeah," I said, "that fame is a relative term. What are you doing?"

"I'm working on Wall Street. You know, I pull in a ton of dough and I'm depressed." He laughed.

"Did you keep up with the writing at all?" I asked.

He shook his head.

The waitress brought the beers. I told him that I'd moved out to Ohio so my wife could get a job she wanted. When he asked what it was like, I said, "Slow as shit. Otherwise, we're out in the country, which is different."

"I'm living in Brooklyn Heights," he said.

I told him that I had to get going because the reading would start in about twenty minutes. He said, "I can't make it, I'm sorry. Would love to see you read a story. It's great to know someone actually got published from that workshop. I'll tell you what, give me the address of the hotel you're staying at. I'll come by late. I gotta go back up to midtown for a meeting with a friend around 11 p.m. I'll stop by your hotel and get you."

I half-heartedly tried to beg off. "I have to split back to Ohio tomorrow," I told him.

"Listen, bud, this woman I'm meeting later is none other than the fiction editor at the *New Yorker.*"

"Get the fuck out of here," I said.

"I'm her broker. You gotta come and meet her."

"I'm pretty sure the fiction editor at the *New Yorker* has no interest in meeting me."

"Trust me, she'll be into it. I'm telling you. She likes all that speculative crap. Really, you should come. She's a million cracks."

As I wrote out the address of my hotel on the back of a matchbook, I asked him, so what's this editor's name?"

"You mean you've never heard of Deb Tresnum?"

I thought for a moment but had to eventually admit I hadn't and shook my head.

"There's only one thing a little freaky about her," he said. "She can't blink. She's got some medical condition that prevents her from blinking. Once an hour, she's gotta put drops in her eyes."

"Sounds bleak," I said.

"Well, it's a little unnerving, but, like I said, she's smooth."

I made it to the KGB with a few minutes to spare and sat on the steps outside smoking a cigarette before heading up the long flight of stairs that led to the bar. While I was sitting there, relaxing, I tried to dredge up some memories of Toby from college. I really didn't remember much about him. What I recalled was his presence on the periphery of parties we'd have, or I could clearly see him reading a story in the workshop. Otherwise, all was unclear. While I had a moment, I took out my phone and texted Barney, whom I'd just stayed with down along the Delaware River. The reason I thought of him was because he'd been in that same fiction workshop in college. I thought maybe he could jog my memory. I left him a quick message on his phone as to where I was and who I'd met.

The reading went off great. I read with a younger writer. He went first, there was a short break, and then I went. There was a good crowd and they seemed to like our stories. I saw a lot of my friends from New York City there. Afterward a bunch of us went out to dinner at a Greek place. I did a lot of drinking—much more than I usually do. Luckily, I kept my wits about me so as to have enough for cab fare on the way back to the hotel. That party broke up around 11. I caught a cab, but when he dropped me off at the Lilliputian Hotel, the driver charged me much more than I thought was right. I thought that fare should have been ten at best, with a tip, but this worked out to a solid fifteen dollars. For a second I was afraid I wasn't going to be able to pay it. The guy didn't take a card. Then I remembered I had a five dollar bill folded four times and stuck into the corner of a secret compartment of my wallet. I was relieved as hell to find it, and being loaded, didn't think twice about using it.

Back in my room, I sat on the bed and stared out the window at the city lights. Something was bothering me. I wasn't so drunk as to feel sick, and my high was starting slowly to wear off. I took my wallet out and opened it and stared into the empty spot where the five had been. It was then that I realized that the meticulously folded five spot had been the protective charm given to me by Averal Braun, the hex doctor. I felt a distinct sinking feeling in my gut and was short of breath. My phone dinged, and I dug it out of my pocket. There was a message from Barney. It read—"Tried to call, no answer. What are you talking about? Toby died during 9/11." Right then, there was a pounding at my room door. I trembled, my mouth went dry, and I could feel my heart chugging.

"Ford, are you in there?" I heard Toby's voice, but now it was a little harsher, a little darker.

The pounding continued, the calling of my name. He got angrier and angrier each time. But I sat where I was, in the dark, my fists clenched, my eyes squeezed shut, and my mind telling me none of this could possibly be happening. That was one morning I did see the dawn.

Harvest

Summer faded, and I willingly turned the air-conditioning off in the second week of October. No more sweating, no more slapping the annoying flies out on the porch. A beautiful wind had come up one night, and I was charmed by the sound of it rattling the dead leaves in the trees. Sitting on the porch alone, a blanket wrapped around my shoulders, Lynn having gone off to bed, I sipped my wine and listened to the ocean-breaker sound the brown foliage in the giant white oak made across the field.

I closed my eyes and rocked and began to doze, when from out in the night there came this horrible raspy moan. I stopped rocking. The cry came again, sounding as if whatever made it was lurking behind the garage. Fin stood up and went to the porch steps as if intending to investigate. I called him to me, and he came and sat next to the rocker. The sound came a third time, and it was loud and hellish like the devil was choking on a sinner's blood. That's exactly the image it conjured in my mind.

I was afraid to get up, afraid to make any movement that might draw it to me. I sat in silence for a minute or so and the night was still again. I thought perhaps the creature had moved off, but then I became concerned because if it moved from behind the garage, my question was, "Where did it move to?" I slowly stood from the rocker and listened intently. Another growl erupted suddenly, and I tossed the blanket back on the chair and ran for the porch door. I was inside in a second. Fin followed me. I slammed it shut. "What the fuck?" I said to the dog.

The very next morning, the cop cars came streaming down the road past the house. It was unusual in that you hardly saw any cars at all on that road, let alone five state troopers. Later, when I went out for cigarettes, I saw that one of the black cars was parked midway down the road at the turnoff for the back way toward town. An officer with a bald head and sunglasses was standing at the corner, holding a shotgun. I stopped and asked him what was going on. As he approached my car, I saw down the two mile stretch of road ahead that there was a trooper car there too with two officers out of the vehicle, one on either side of the road.

"What's up?" I asked.

The cop said, "They had a detail of prisoners out on the side of Rt. 70 cleaning up this morning and one of them made a break. We're pretty sure he's held up in one of these cornfields around here. You live up the road?"

"Yeah," I said.

"Keep your doors locked and give us a call if you notice anything."

"Will do," I said. "Thanks for the rundown."

"We'll catch him," said the cop.

Famous last words, 'cause they didn't catch him. By the next afternoon, the story of the runaway convict was all over the local news and had made it to CNN online. There were cop cars all over the roads between the fields—sheriff's department, U.S. Marshals, local town cops, state troopers. When I went out for butts, I saw they had tracking dogs they were leading into the cornfields. There was a helicopter circling about. What I learned on the radio was that the convict had been in the army special forces and had training to survive outside on his own, and that's why the authorities were having such a hard time getting him. He knew how to throw the dogs off or hide in culverts, stay ahead of his pursuers. They believed he was still right in our general area. For all I knew, he could have been holed up in the old shed in our yard.

There was a week and a half before the corn would come down, and if they didn't have him by then, they'd have to get him as there'd be no place left to hide. I sat in the back in the cool weather, wearing a hooded sweatshirt, writing at my little table in the orchard. Every once and a while, I'd look up and out across the cornfield beyond our property to see if there was anything large moving through the rows. The corn had all gone utterly brown and almost clacked together in the wind it was so dry. Since it was feed corn and corn for industry, the farmers waited till absolutely all of the sugar had been drained from the plant into the ears.

I wasn't fearful about the convict—that is until one day when my son and his girlfriend came over to visit. We sat on the porch and drank coffee, and Brianna, Jack's girlfriend, who'd grown up in town, told me that she knew the guy who had escaped into the cornfields. She was in the high school class just a year later than his.

"He was always a crazy fucker," she said.

"You mean that guy was from around here?" I asked.

"Oh yeah. Jem Nelson."

"A bad character?" I asked.

"Not so much bad as just weird. A loner. He finally went away and joined the army. He was over in Afghanistan, sneaking around and cutting throats. What do they call it, a ranger or Special Forces? He came back and never really fit in. Then they arrested him a little while ago for killing some guy back on Morgan Road. He was loaded or high on something and he drove the guy off the road with his truck."

"Wait a second," I said. "Are you talking about a black pickup truck?"

"Yeah, that guy," said Brianna and laughed. "Did you ever get in front of him on the road?"

"Jesus, yeah."

Later on, when Jack and Brianna went back to their apartment in town, I went around and locked all the doors and windows. Lynn was away on a business trip and was due to be gone all week. I was petrified that Jem Nelson would surface in the backyard and try to force his way into the house at night. He already seemed to have something against me, or something had something against me. Trying to sort out the threads of magic and hex and plain old madness was impossible. I kept a big butcher knife, sort of like a kitchen machete, handy whenever I had to go out at night to take a bag of garbage to the can. I stayed off the porch, and when it was time for Fin to go out for a piss at the end of the night, I put him on the chain so he couldn't go too far.

Eventually the harvest started, and the farmers began dismantling the rows of corn. Over a period of a few days the vast fields were mowed and all of the bounty of the summer months was stored away. The cops were on hand for the entire thing, dogs at the ready to give chase when Jem Nelson lost his cover and ran for it. The U.S. Marshals went door to door and checked everyone's outbuildings and sheds. To my surprise and theirs, they never found the guy. In my garage as well as the one next door and one around the corner owned by the Mennonites, they did find evidence that he'd probably stayed in those structures during the colder nights of the manhunt. The officers showed me there was a dead animal in the back of my garage. They pulled it out and laid it on the ground. It was a red fox.

"I don't understand," I said. "Why would he leave that in my garage?"

"You can't eat the animal. Well, you can, but you've got to marinate it for a long time and it is really gamey and tough eating. And you've got to boil it extensively. But you can eat the tongue after cooking it over a direct flame for a few minutes," said the officer. "And that's what he did here," he said, pointing at the dead animal. Its coat was beautiful and its tail fluffy. Nelson had used some of my old manuscript pages he'd dug out of a box to start the fire he used to cook it.

"It's a little sustenance, and a little sustenance goes a long way when you're on the lam," said the Marshal.

"Seems a horrible waste," I said. "So where is he now?"

"Most of the fields are down, and he's not been spotted from the helicopter. We've checked pretty much every building he could possibly be holed up in. I guess he slipped the net and has moved on. We'll get him eventually."

But they never did.

The fact that he had been in the garage freaked me more than a little. A few days after the police had given up the stake-out, I was out there straightening things up in the spot where the escapee had hidden. On the concrete floor, between two boxes, I found the root figure the history student had dug up over the summer. I had no idea how it had gotten there. I tried to wonder what path it had taken to find its way to my garage, but every avenue I daydreamed boggled my mind beyond comprehension. The night before Lynn got back, I burned the little effigy. It snap, crackled, popped, and I made sure it turned to ash. On a night of a full moon and Venus glowing brightly on the horizon, I buried the ashes out amid the roots of the white oak.

Acknowledgments

Thanks to all the editors who helped to make these stories better in their initial incarnations: Ellen Datlow, Navah Wolfe, Dominik Parisien, Bradford Morrow, Charlie Finlay, Eric Guignard, Gavin J. Grant, Kelly Link.

Publication History

"The Thousand Eyes," *The Starlit Wood: New Fairy Tales,* 2016
"Hibbler's Minions," *Nightmare Carnival,* 2014
"Monster Eight," *Conjunctions* 74, 2020
"Inn of the Dreaming Dog," "Monkey in the Woods," and "The Match" appear here for the first time.
"From the Balcony of the Idawolf Arms," *Final Cuts,* 2020
"Sisyphus in Elysium," *The Mythic Dream,* 2019
"The Jeweled Wren," *Echoes: The Saga Anthology of Ghost Stories,* 2019
"Not Without Mercy," *Conjunctions* 67, 2016
"The Bookcase Expedition," *Robots VS. Fairies,* 2018
"The Winter Wraith," in *The Magazine of Fantasy & Science Fiction,* 2015
"Big Dark Hole," *Conjunctions* 71, 2018
"Thanksgiving," *The Magazine of Fantasy & Science Fiction,* 2018
"The Five Pointed Spell," *Horror Library* #6, 2017

About the Author

Jeffrey Ford was born on Long Island in New York State in 1955 and grew up in the town of West Islip. He studied fiction writing with John Gardner at S.U.N.Y Binghamton. He's been a college English teacher of writing and literature for thirty years. He is the author of nine novels, including *The Girl in the Glass* and five short story collections, including *A Natural History of Hell.* He has received multiple World Fantasy and Shirley Jackson awards as well as the Nebula and Edgar awards, among others. He lives with his wife, Lynn, in a century-old farmhouse in a land of slow clouds and endless fields.

ALSO AVAILABLE FROM SMALL BEER PRESS

TRADE PAPER 9781618730602 | EBOOK 9781618730619

SHIRLEY JACKSON AWARD WINNER
WORLD FANTASY AWARD AND BRAM STOKER AWARD FINALIST
ADAPTED INTO THE HULU TV SERIES MONSTERLAND

"Pain is one of the most private experiences people face, and yet a universal experience. *North American Lake Monsters* uses this palette to create most of its narrative hues and textures, to sharpen and heighten the characteristics of its profoundly human, deeply flawed characters." — *Toronto Globe and Mail*

ALSO AVAILABLE FROM SMALL BEER PRESS

TRADE PAPER 9781618731180 | EBOOK 9781618731197

WORLD FANTASY & SHIRLEY JACKSON AWARD WINNER
OHIOANA BOOK & LOCUS AWARD FINALIST

★ "Seamlessly blends subtle psychological horror with a mix of literary history, folklore, and SF in this collection of 13 short stories, all focused on the struggles, sorrows, and terrors of daily life." — *Publishers Weekly* (starred review)

"Delivers plenty of black humor and bone-dry social satire."
—Jason Heller, NPR